mad

a short story about love and mermaids

sea

K WEBSTER

BOOKS BY AUTHOR K WEBSTER

"Go on and kiss the girl."
– Sebastian, *The Little Mermaid*

dedication

To my husband.

My love for you is deeper than the deep blue sea,

you see.

A Note to the Reader:

Mad Sea was originally created as a story for an anthology. There were size constraints which explains the short length of this story. Because of this, the story is sweet, to the point, and all kinds of instalove. If you're looking for a quick, lovable read that is quite outside your normal reading zone, then you're going to love this.

I've been dying to write a story about mermaids and I've finally been able to scratch that itch. It has something for everyone…a motorcycle gang full of dirty talkin' alphas, sexy mermaids, voyeuristic dolphins, and sweet love!

I hope you enjoy reading this as much as I enjoyed writing it!

Sincerely,
K Webster

"Little cherub of the sea, come and play with me.
Come and play with me, dearest cherub of the sea.
Please come play with me,
In the mad, mad sea."

chapter one

Madden

FOR THE MOST PART, MEMBERS OF AN OUTLAW motorcycle club are badass motherfuckers. Leather wearing, tattoo sportin', weapon toting, hell raising kind of guys. They push drugs and fuck as much as they drink. And they fight nearly as much as they eat. Bikers have a reputation for being rough around the edges and crude. Illegal activities are their game of choice and rebellion is their middle name. They rule the streets with their hogs between their thighs and murderous glares on their rugged faces. They are outlaws.

And I lead the gang.

The ring fucking leader.

Mr. Badass himself.

Every day we ride. On Tuesdays, I head to the shipyards so I can oversee our weapons import. Thursdays, I taste from the newest strain of cocaine that will get cut for distribution. Saturdays, I collect on my debts.

But Sundays…

Sundays are *my* day.

My fucking day off.

"The usual, sir?"

I snap my head up from staring at the tips of my worn leather boots and meet the pale green eyes of Hali Morgan. Her strawberry-blonde hair has been pulled back into a sleek ponytail today, like always, and her lips are glossy pink. I'd rather taste *her* instead of what I'm here for, but she doesn't even know my fucking name.

"Yes," I say with a grunt. "Thank you, Hali."

She beams at me, flashing her perfect white teeth, and punches in some numbers on the register. "That'll be five-oh-nine, sir."

Here's the deal. I've been coming to see her every Sunday for three months. Three fucking months. I'm pussy whipped by a register girl who doesn't even know my name.

But her?

I know everything the internet yields regarding Hali Elaine Morgan. She's not big on Facebook but is always posting shit on Instagram. Not self-absorbed selfies. Not my Hali. Naw, she's more into scenery and sunsets. Shells and palm trees. Muscle cars and puffy clouds. I know this because my stupid ass created a fake profile just to inconspicuously follow her. I try not to go full-on creeper and like every single picture she posts. Currently, I've kept my liking to every other post.

I'm a stalker *and* a pussy.

Jesus fucking Christ.

If only the guys back at the clubhouse knew this, they'd be slitting my throat and electing a new president before sundown. My best friend, Jagger, and that fucktard Cassius, wouldn't even wait until my body was cold before one of them was sitting in my place at the head of the table.

"Sir?"

I snap out of my daze and shove my hand into my black jeans. Pulling out a ten dollar bill, I slap it on the counter. "Keep the change, sweetheart."

Her pale, freckled cheeks tinge pink as she slides the bill from me. "Thank you."

When she bounces off to make my order, I run my fingers through my jet black hair in frustration. At the clubhouse, all I have to do is look at one of the broads sitting on one of the worn sofas and they'll be sucking my cock in three seconds flat.

But Hali?

I can't even talk to her without feeling like I'm a fourteen-year-old nerdy little shit. It's emasculating and embarrassing, yet I keep coming back here. Every goddamned Sunday for more punishment.

My gaze travels over to her. Her head is bopping to the music on the speakers—some Justin Timberlake crap—and her supple lips mouth the words as she pulls a cup from the dispenser. Then, she bounces over to the frozen yogurt machine and pulls the lever. Bubblegum flavored frozen yogurt fills the cup, but I'm too focused on how delicious her ass looks in her tiny white shorts to notice her actions. It's the best damn part of my week. What I wouldn't give to pull out my flaying knife and slice them right from her ripe, tight body.

She casts a shy glance my way over her shoulder and smiles before mounting on the toppings. Pink sprinkles. Pink gummy worms. Pink dyed coconut flakes.

Yes, I am the loser who orders this shit.

When she shoves a lime green spoon into the frozen yogurt, she turns, scoops up a matching green napkin along the way and bounces back over to me. I'd die to have her bouncing on my cock instead.

"The Pink Pelican," she chirps and winks at me. "A Franny Froyo fave!"

An elderly lady chuckles from behind me in line, and I cringe. "Thanks."

When she passes the cup to me, I deliberately touch her soft, small hands and thank God for the counter hiding my hard-on. This girl does things to me.

"Ask her out already, son," the old woman orders. "Your tongue is on the floor and the gal looks like she might want to be the one to roll it back up for you."

I clench my teeth and flash Hali an apologetic look. "I'm, uh…"

"At least tell her your name," the nosy lady gripes.

Hali giggles, a sound lighter and more musical than any wind chime my adopted mother, Constance, ever collected, and I instantly crave more of it. Every day. On repeat. Jesus.

"Madden Finn. My friends call me Mad."

Hali grins at me. "Pleasure to finally make your acquaintance, Mad. See you around."

Feeling like a dick, I stalk away from the sniggering old woman and find my usual lime green plastic chair by the window. I have a perfect view of both my love, the sea, *and* my obsession, Froyo Hali.

As I eat a dessert that makes me feel more like a woman than a man, I catch my reflection in the mirrored glass along the far wall. I don't fucking belong here. All six feet and five inches of solid muscle, with a leather jacket too hot for Miami make me stand out like a sore thumb. My black hair is a wild mess, matching the emotions running rampant in my head. Eyes, so black they're nearly blue, peer back at me.

Angry.

Possessive.

Unapproachable.

Fucking terrifying.

I'm surprised half the town doesn't run in the other direction when they see me. Truth is, they mostly do. Aside from my Sunday visits at the frozen yogurt stand on the beach where I turn in my mancard and balls the second the bell on the door jingles. Here, I'm some ridiculous fool.

After another week of disappointment, I toss my empty container into the trash can and stalk out of the restaurant toward my bike without a backwards glance at my shiny, pretty obsession.

"All you have to do is ask, you know. I won't bite," a sweet voice says with a chuckle from behind me as I straddle my machine. "Well, I won't bite that hard."

I snap my head to the vision gracefully making her way over to me. "Ask what?" I grunt.

Unafraid of my gruff exterior, she sashays right up to me and invades my personal space. I'm about three seconds from hauling her onto this bike with me and taking her home.

"Ask in the next five seconds, and the answer will be yes. Ask me after, and it will be no."

With her out of the yuppie froyo shop, I'm a little more in my element. I flash her a smug grin. "Will you marry me?"

Her green eyes widen with surprise, and she giggles. "Oooh, you're a sly one, Madden Finn. Here I thought you were shy but no, you knew exactly what you were doing!"

I can't help but laugh with her—it's infectious and I want to be tainted by her. "We'll deal with that answer later. Can I take you to dinner one night?"

"I suppose so," she says, "a girl has to eat." She hands me a green napkin with her phone number written in a pretty flourish across the front. "Text me and let me know when."

With a wave, she turns and starts away from me, but I'm quick and snatch her wrist. It's tiny in my massive hand and I easily bring her toward me. I don't say anything but press a soft kiss to her palm that smells like dessert toppings.

"I've been waiting twelve Sundays to do that."

I release her and keep my eyes on her as she hurries back into the building, her round ass jiggling as she bounces away.

One day soon, I'll make this girl mine.

Once the engine roars to life and I'm back on the road, the warm wind whipping around me, I contemplate how any sort of relationship with a girl like Hali would work. In all actuality, it can't. I'm hardened and rough. She's all sweetness and smooth perfection. And one step inside the clubhouse, those motherfuckers would devour my sweet treat.

Fuck that. I'll figure out a way to have both. I'm a master at compartmentalizing my life. My adopted mother and her cats, who I still visit frequently at her beach house, are in a safe, secret compartment that only Jagger knows about. My Sunday visits with Hali are another part of me no one knows a thing about. And the biggest piece of me, stays in its own undisclosed part of my mind.

I pull into the carport of my condo on the beach. The clubhouse may be the place I run, but I don't live there. Instead, I stay at the worn two bedroom condo that's fairly private, with no beachgoers out my way. Turning off the motorcycle, I climb off and head straight toward the water, shedding leather and denim along the way. Boots are kicked off and my weapons are discarded into the sand without a care in the world.

As soon as I'm completely naked and standing before my true home, I smile and inhale the salty breeze.

Could I ever share this part of me with anyone?

Maybe someone like Hali?

What would she think of me?

A growl rumbles in my throat just thinking of her rejection—the horror on her face from knowing exactly who, or more like *what* I am. She can't ever know. It'll remain in its compartment where it belongs.

I charge toward the raging waves and once I'm waist deep, I dive in. The water sluices down my bare skin, sending a calm like no other washing over me. Closing my eyes, I will the change to happen. Over the years, I've learned to control when I convert into my true form.

My legs begin binding together, almost painfully, but I don't feel trapped. I know it's the step before I become truly free. The tightening becomes more and more intense with each passing second, as if some heavenly god is sewing my powerful legs together against my will. I fight the urge to gasp for air and claw to the surface, but instead suck the saltwater deep into my lungs. The water is murky, but I know soon I'll be able to see, with crystal clarity, everything in the sea.

Everything goes black for one quiet moment.

Then, underwater, brilliant colors nearly blind me. Colorful fish dart around me and the peaceful sounds of the ocean soothe my soul.

I'm free.

With a powerful whap of my tail, I surge deeper

into the ocean. Being in my true form, I'm strong and untouchable. I'm free to search every salty square inch of the sea for others like me. Every evening, I do just that. I spend hours swimming and hunting for a family I never knew.

But as exhilarating as this is, it's also lonely.

It's like I'm the last one of an extinct race.

Alone.

After hours of getting my fill, I come across a shimmering, red tinted shell with green speckles in it. It instantly reminds me of Hali.

Maybe one day I can share who I am with someone. If anything, a sweet girl like Hali would be the one to accept such an unusual notion about someone. Gritting my teeth, I start making my swim back toward shore. Of course I can't tell her. If I like her, which I really fucking do, I can't tell her that…ever.

How fucking ridiculous would that be?

"Hi, my name is Madden Finn, president of the South Beach Sinners and Pink Pelican frozen yogurt eating yuppie. Oh…" I groan as I clutch the shell in my fist, drawing blood. "And I'm a fucking merman."

chapter two

Hali

"**D**OES THE NEW BOYFRIEND KNOW YOU'RE A hooker?" Steffan questions from the couch, a puff of smoke clouding the air around him.

I bristle at his comment and halt in my tracks. When I moved to Miami, I didn't have a nickel to my name. I'd been lost and on the run from crap I'd rather not think about. While searching for not only a job but a place to put down some roots, I'd come across Steffan. He'd been at the bus station just standing there, waiting, when our eyes locked. His blue eyes, the color of the sky on the clearest of days, had found mine and he claimed me. Simple as that. I'd found my feet walking his way as he lit up a cigarette. He'd asked me questions about my intentions in this town, told me his, and soon, I found myself following him to his apartment.

We didn't have sex.

Not that he hasn't tried on the occasional drunk night.

But we became bonded in an unexplainable way. He became my only friend. My caretaker. The one who gave me a roof over my head and a pillow to lie my head upon. To me, he's like an annoying, nosy older brother. Stalker should be a more appropriate word, but I give him the benefit of the doubt. Always. Because even when he's regarding me with his cold gaze, I always see a flicker of warmth beyond his frigid façade. He may hate the world and everyone in it, but with me, he shows a flicker of love. Be it that it's small, it's still there. And I'm grateful for his flicker. I protect it from the harsh gusts of the world around us and it keeps me warm.

"Screw you," I huff and storm over to him. "You seriously don't understand the meaning of privacy."

He shrugs his shoulders as if it's not a big deal. But looking at my phone while I'm asleep, or in the shower, is such an invasion of privacy. If I didn't love him like a brother, I'd have left him long ago.

"You're pissed about me reading your texts, but you have no argument for the fact that I just called you a fucking prostitute. I guess my suspicions were correct," he says with a disgusted snarl and stands. He runs his fingers through his overgrown, dark blond hair and pins me with an angry scowl.

I hate when he's like this. When his mind comes up with impossible scenarios—all fucked up and twisted. All scenarios that involve me being pulled into the dark underworld.

"I know you don't mean it," I tell him in a calm voice and try to meet his angry gaze with my own. "Madden's just a guy I met at Franny's. He asked me to dinner. Seemed like a nice guy and you know I'm always hungry," I tease.

He frowns, and sadness flickers across his features before he hardens his look. "I feed you. I'm the one who takes care of you."

"You've always looked after me, ever since we met two years ago. I can't thank you enough for that, Steff." I approach him like one would an injured animal. Once I'm close enough, I fold myself into his arms. He grips me in a tight embrace. "You're my best friend. But you have to let me spread my wings a bit."

A growl rumbles in his chest, and he stiffens. "The world is a terrible place. They'll hurt you. The whole lot of them."

I smile against his chest. "I'll be fine. It's one date."

"If he hurts you, I'll put a bullet in him."

"And I'll put a bullet in you if you don't let me get ready for said date. It's just dinner, and I'll be home before you know it. If he's an ass, I give you permission to kick his ass. Deal?"

He grunts. I'm thinking no deal.

"Oh, and if you keep snooping on my phone, I'm going to kick your ass into tomorrow. Got it, bud?" I threaten with a laugh.

I pull away and make my way into my bedroom. I'll need a quick shower before my date. I'm just peeling off my tank top and tossing it onto the floor when I feel his presence behind me.

"What's your deal today?" I hiss and grab a towel to cover my bare chest.

He's leaned against the doorframe, his bright blue eyes devouring my half naked appearance. "Where have you been?"

Always the same song and dance with us. He wants answers. Answers I don't want to give. Sometimes a girl needs her privacy. And Steffan makes it really freaking hard to be private.

"I went shopping out by the piers. Looking for something to wear tonight."

His eyes narrow and his jaw clenches. Just when I think he'll interrogate me some more, he storms off.

Once I save some money up, I really need to consider getting my own place. Steffan is bordering on creepy these days. It'll save our friendship if I leave him before I kill him.

I flip through my phone while I wait for Madden to show up. He'd offered to pick me up, but I didn't think it was a good idea for Steffan to see him. Instead, I told him I'd meet him at the Seaside Steakhouse. Men and women keep entering the busy place, donning expensive dresses and suits. I frown, wondering if I've underdressed for the evening.

For my date, I'd chosen a white halter top dress that hits me at my knees. White sandals were my shoes of choice, and I spent entirely too long attempting to put curls in my hair. In the end, my strawberry-blonde ringlets fell into beachy waves. Damn humidity.

I'm about to check the time on my phone when I sense his presence. Just like every Sunday at work, I know it's him when he walks in without even having to look up. Madden has a powerful aura about him. His smell is an intoxicating manly scent—a delicious mixture of ocean water and leather. I can always feel his eyes on me, like a tongue lazily dragging its way along my flesh. A shiver courses through me and my skin is sprinkled with goosebumps.

"Did I keep you waiting long?" his deep voice rumbles from behind me.

I stand from the bench and turn to see him leaning against one of the pillars in front of the building. Tonight he's dressed differently than usual. Gone are the leather and denim. Now, he's dressed in a pair of grey slacks that fit his muscular frame nicely and a black button-up dress shirt with the top few buttons undone and the sleeves rolled up to just below his elbows, showcasing his firm forearms. His black hair is a styled mess on top of his head. The man is sex personified.

"No, not at all," I say, grinning at the handsome man.

Our texts had been simple, the two of us deciding on a time and place. My fingers itched to probe him. To ask him a million questions about himself, but I decided to save it for our date.

He walks over to me, his gaze hungry almost, until he's towering over me. Another shiver ripples through me when he dips his head and sniffs me. Yes, sniffs. Normally, I'd be offended, but this time I can't help but hope I smell good enough to eat.

"You look fucking amazing," he growls, not moving away from my personal space. "I'm not really good at this whole dating thing. Right now, all of my thoughts involve you, and none of them are the least bit respectful."

I lift my chin and meet his darkened eyes. Lifting an eyebrow at him in question, I smile. "To be honest, I'm not good at this whole dating thing either. So maybe we can navigate this together. I'm not entirely opposed to coming up with our own way of doing things."

He grins, flashing me his bright white teeth, and I wonder what it would feel like to have them nibbling on me. When I shiver again, he brings his massive palms to my bare arms and runs them up and down along the flesh to warm me back up.

"Want to ditch this fancy shit and do something different?" he questions, his head nodding to the restaurant.

I laugh. "It's like you read my mind. There're some food trucks down by the pier. Want to grab some food from one of those?"

He takes my hand, firm but gentle, and guides me away from the restaurant. The walk to the food trucks is about a mile, but we aren't in a hurry.

"So," I say with a chuckle, "how exactly does a guy like you end up in a frozen yogurt place. Do you really like frozen yogurt, or do you come to see me?"

His hand squeezes mine, and I swear he growls. The deep rumble excites me. "I saw you walking in one day and wanted to know you. You're not like the other women I've been around. It was refreshing. I had to know you."

I turn my head to find him staring straight ahead. His blatant honesty makes my heart thunder in my chest.

"I'm glad you did. You're certainly different than any other man I've encountered," I tell him.

He stops and reaches for my other hand. Once he's pulled me in front of him, he peers down at me. "You have no idea just how different I am, Hali. I'm probably the worst kind of guy you could ever get wrapped up with. That should stop me. I should walk away and pretend I never saw you." I frown at his words. "But I can't. There's something about you that calls to me. I'm different around you. If my friends could see me, they'd think I was a pussy. I won't lie to you though, beautiful. I'm a bad man."

His eyebrows furrow in frustration at his admission. It makes me want to hug him. So I do. As soon as I tug my hands from his and wrap my arms around his middle, something happens. I'm dizzied by our connection. He squeezes me to him and kisses my hair, also doing that inhaling thing I like so much again.

"Why are you hugging me?" he questions in a huff, almost as if he's angry at himself for asking.

"Because you looked like you needed one."

"Now I don't want to let you go."

I smile against his chest. "So don't."

His fingers run through my wavy hair, and he groans. "Did you hear that part about where I'm a bad man but I crave you and can't seem to stay away? That I'm bad news?"

Lifting my chin to meet his stare, I inspect his features. He's beautiful. God wouldn't create such a magnificent creature and make him evil. Not possible.

"Then out with it. Tell me what it is you think I'll run from."

He sighs. "I'm the president of a motorcycle club. We aren't the friendly Sunday riders type either. Drugs, weapons, crime…it's a norm for me, Hali. I don't want that world to touch you, though. I'd like to show you I'm more than that."

I consider his words. "So tell me the more."

"Well, I'm an avid swimmer. The ocean is my second home—the place where I feel most comfortable. I hate seafood and won't touch the shit with a ten foot pole. My adopted mother is a wind chime freak and loves cats. About once a month, I go on a hunt for a wind chime she doesn't have. Something unique and wonderful like her. I'm a huge rock music fan. And apparently, I'm a froyo yuppie on Sundays."

We both laugh. I like the way the moonlight makes his eyes dance with mischief.

"Sounds like you live two lives," I say thoughtfully, understanding how he feels. "And you want to know me in one of them."

His eyes close, but he nods. "Essentially, yes. Not that I am embarrassed of you. Fuck that. You're just too sweet and pure for that other world."

While his eyes are still closed, I stand on my toes and press a kiss to the corner of his mouth. "Maybe I'm not so sweet."

He threads his fingers into my hair and tugs gently until my lips part open. When his full lips descend upon mine, I let out an eager moan. It's been ages since I've kissed anyone. Far too long. The moment our lips connect, his tongue is on a search for mine. I like his taste, minty and clean. It doesn't take long before I'm desperately trying to taste all of him. His teeth find my bottom lip and he nibbles me before diving back into our kiss. I'm embarrassingly needy for his kiss. So close to climbing his body like a tree.

"Come on, beautiful," he murmurs breathlessly as he tears away from our kiss. "Let's get something to eat before we devour each other instead."

mad sea

We'd bought some gyros and Cokes before settling to sit at the end of a pier, our legs dangling. After we inhaled our meal and Madden disposed of the trash, he sat back down beside me.

"Now tell me about you. What's your story?" he questions, his arm wrapping around me from behind.

I lean into his warmth. My gut begs for me to gift him with the stories of my past. To slice myself open and show him what makes me, me. But I've worked too hard to put the past behind me. I've created a life here in Miami that doesn't involve my over-protective father and his insane wishes for me. Here, I'm me. Hali Morgan. Here, I don't have to follow rules.

"Just working at the yogurt place until I can get my photography going. I've been taking classes on the side. One day, I'd love to make money doing what I love. I thought it would be neat to take pictures for postcards for a gift shop or something. Hadn't really thought exactly what I'll do, but my heart lies, like yours, with the beach and ocean. I feel at peace here."

He reaches into his pocket and pulls something out. "After you agreed to our date, I found this. Reminded me of you." When he opens his palm, I gasp. In it is a beautiful shell—reds and greens shimmering in the moonlight.

"I love it," I murmur as I take it from him. He watches me as I turn it over in my hand and run my thumb along the grooves. "This type of shell isn't found often on the beach. That was a lucky find, Madden."

I'm eager to get it in the sunlight and take some pictures of it. Once I safely tuck it away in my purse, I turn to look at him. His expression is serious as he devours me with his gaze.

"I want to kiss you again," he states plainly, the corner of his mouth quirking up into a half smile that looks incredibly good on him.

I bat my eyelashes at him. "So kiss me."

His palm finds my jaw and he guides me to him for another kiss. After only a moment of his tongue in my mouth, I am already craving more from him. This is exactly why my father and I butted heads. He had a plan for me that didn't involve desire or connection or love. It was all about power and status. Nothing I cared about.

"More," I moan, mostly to myself.

He drags me into his lap, and I straddle him while we kiss. It drives me wild knowing he's hard for me. As I grind against his erection, I begin to wonder how big he is. If he's good in the sack. Is he a generous lover? I'm not that experienced. Once, Steffan's cousin who was in town, ended up going down on me after one too many vodka shots. My roommate never knew, thank God. It was interesting, but not necessarily satisfying. That's where my experience ends. Alyssa, my friend from back home, once told me sex isn't worth it until you're with someone worth having sex with. She'd been with a ton of guys. Her tune changed once she met Alec. I hadn't really wanted to sleep with anyone, until now. Hadn't ever really even thought about it much.

Madden's large hands grip my ass through my dress and he pushes me against him, clearly needing the friction as much as I do. If there weren't people at the end of the pier, I'm afraid I might turn into a whore and beg him to fuck me right here. I'm getting turned on by that image when I'm attacked.

By a moth.

A stupid fucking moth.

"Get it off of me!" I screech as I sit ramrod straight and swat at the thing that's bigger than any damn butterfly I've ever seen.

Madden's rich laughter warms me until the thing attacks my face again. My first instinct is to push away. And away I go.

The fall from the pier seems to go in slow motion. My eyes fixate on the moon above me, and I wonder if the moth is still hunting me. I'm torn from my thoughts the moment my back makes impact with the cool water. Fire whips across my backside. Before I can regain my bearings, a wave rushes over me and pulls me under.

I'm still dazzled by the fall, so I don't realize I'm under water until two strong arms wrap around my waist an instant later. As soon as he touches me, my flesh erupts in a sensation I've never felt before. It's like his soul is slithering from his body and enveloping mine. I'm dizzied by the unusual feeling. It's erotic and exotic. I like the addictive way it feels.

"Relax, I've got you," he murmurs against the shell of my ear as he swims us to shore.

I'm an excellent swimmer, but right now, I'm

enjoying being rescued by this god of a man. I've probably ruined our date. A part of me should be sad at the notion. But all I can think about is how much better our date got, now that his body is molded against mine.

As soon as we reach the shore, he scoops me into his arms and carries me to a sand dune. He sets me down to regard me with concerned eyes. His black shirt is pressed against his muscled chest, making me crazy with the need to peel it from his body.

"Stay here. I'm going to fetch your purse, my phone and wallet, and my shoes. I'll be right back." His lips find mine for a moment, and then he's gone.

I watch him as he trots off, his toned ass flexing with each stride. If I hadn't have fallen in, I'd have missed his beautiful butt and how it looks in a soaked pair of slacks.

This date is definitely one I won't ever forget.

chapter three

Madden

I LET HER FALL.

She was in my arms, and I let her go.

A growl rumbles in my chest, anger crackling through me like bolts of lightning in a storm, as I carry her purse back to where she's still sprawled out on her back staring up at the moon. Hali could have broken her neck or fucking drowned. Unbelievable.

"I'm sorry our date is ruined." Disgust is thick in my voice. I fall to my ass in the sand and look down at her. Her brows are furled together.

"Because of me?" Her bottom lip wobbles for a brief moment and all anger fades away. Now, I want to kiss away whatever is making her sad.

"Fuck no. Because of me. I should have held onto you. You could have been killed, woman."

"Come here," she whispers lowly, almost low enough I can't hear her. "I need to tell you something."

I stretch out beside her and lean toward her face. She smiles in a wicked way that has my dick hardening as she clutches onto my wet shirt. I'm yanked to her mouth where our lips, once again, fuse together as if they were meant to do so.

I'm actually addicted to this woman.

Her taste, still sweet from the Coke, is one I'll never forget. When I pull away to look down at her, I can't help the smile tugging at my lips. "What were you going to tell me?"

She flits her fingers along my jawline and threads them in my hair. Her green orbs shimmer in the moonlight. "This date is perfect. I've been coasting along for two years. Lonely and bored. Aside from my photography and my roommate, nothing has really excited me. You, Madden Finn, excite me."

Her chest heaves, and I flicker my gaze to her nipples that are standing at attention under her white dress. I'd give anything for the chance to pull away her wet dress and suck one into my mouth. But, I'm trying something new with this girl. She's not one of the dumb clubhouse bitches.

Hali is unique.

And I want to keep her as mine.

Fucking treasure her.

"Come on," I say with a grumble. "I'll drive you home before you get sick."

Her eyes widen. "On the motorcycle?"

Laughing, I shake my head. "Too dangerous for you, beautiful. You get to ride in the Jeep."

She pouts, which makes her all the damn cuter.

How will I ever be able to compartmentalize this girl?

I'm going to want her all of the time.

"New guy," Jagger grunts as he climbs off his bike. "Ramone fucking vanished."

My guard is up the moment we arrive at the abandoned factory that backs up to the ocean. Ramone usually meets us here with the newest shipment of cocaine, fresh from Columbia. Before we headed over here, I got a text from someone new. Javier. He'd said he was taking over the business. I told my boys to be alert and ready in case any shit goes down.

"You Javier?" My voice echoes inside the large metal building, now that our bikes aren't thundering any longer.

The man with dark hair and a goatee nods. "Javier Ramirez. I can assure you, business will go as usual."

It agitates me that he's so sure I will want to continue to do business with him. One thing will determine how that goes. The cocaine. Ramone knew his shit and he was honest. Both go a long way in the drug world.

"Let's see what you're pushing," I say as I stride over to him. He's got a table set up with a bag sitting on top.

He gestures with a wolfish grin that has my hackles on alert. "Sample the product. Columbian perfection."

Jagger saunters past me. The massive guy is intimidating as hell with a shaved head, neck tattoos, and a perpetual scowl. Javier isn't immune to Jagger's intimidation and his eyes become shifty as he watches my friend approach the coke. Jagger dips his finger into the white powder and tastes it. Cassius follows behind him. When Cassius's shoulders tense, I cut my eyes to Jagger. His gaze flits over to the pallet filled with boxes labeled as flour. Nodding, understanding his message, I make my way over to the table with the coke they just sampled to see for myself what the problem is.

It's okay.

Not Ramone quality.

"Trust goes a long way with the Southside Sinners. Am I right, Cass?" My eyes remain fixed on Javier. Cassius grunts and stalks over to the pallet.

"That it does, Mad Dog." He yanks his pocket knife out and cuts open the first box.

"It's the same," Javier assures me, his palms in the air. Despite his assurances, I don't trust the guy.

Jagger walks over to help Cassius. Together, they pull the boxes out, one by one. They're silent as they cut open each box and sample the goods. Javier has since paled, but wisely remains quiet.

"Well?" I question, my eyes still on Javier.

"No deal." Cassius's angry glare meets mine, and I nod my understanding.

With the force of a hurricane Miami hasn't

even seen before, I slam my fist into Javier's face. The man crumples to his knees, clutching his now bleeding nose.

"Stupid American!" he cries out.

My boys and I all start back toward our bikes. We leave the scammer asshole with his shitty coke to head back to the clubhouse. As soon as we're inside, I motion for them to follow me into my office for a meeting. Several club whores smile seductively at me as we pass, but I ignore them all. I yearn to think about her. Hali Morgan. The one who continuously plagues my thoughts. However, I'm working hard at keeping her in a safe place where she belongs. Even thinking about her in this environment is detrimental to her safety.

"What are we gonna do, boss?" Steam, a big 'ol boy with a white beard that resembles Santa's, questions as he settles on the bench at the table.

I take my place at the head and regard all of the rough men as they sit. "What do our finances look like, Moe?"

Moe, before losing his wife and kids in a car accident, was an accountant at one time. After the most devastating time of his life, he joined our motorcycle club and became our numbers boy. He's good at what he does. We've plenty of investments to keep us funded for years.

"Depends on what you want to do, Mad Dog. I don't want to work with that lying shithead though. That'll just fuck things up on our end with our clientele," he says with a groan.

He leaves the room briefly and returns with the ledger. One of the club bitches comes in to ask if anyone wants a drink. Once we're all settled with a cold beer, Moe looks up from his paperwork.

"We don't need it. The stocks are performing well and the mutual funds aren't losing. There's enough to pay all the bills and keep things moving comfortably. Hell, we could even drop the arms dealing altogether for three years and five months. We'd still have enough to last that long, operating with all of our assets."

Cassius grunts his irritation, but it's Jagger who surprises me with his anger.

"So that's just it, man? Give it all up and fucking retire for three years?" His brown eyes flicker with rage.

I roll my eyes at him and cross my arms over my chest. "Nobody said anything about quitting, fuckwad. We're just exploring our options. Let's keep weapons going like normal. For now, we're going to bow out of all drug dealings. Cass, you stay on the hunt for a new distributor. Find out what the fuck happened to Ramone."

My phone beeps in my pocket indicating a text. Everything in me craves to pull it out and read it. Unfortunately, I'm in a bathtub full of sharks. One whiff of something sweet like her, and it will be a frenzy to the death to see who can devour her first.

"Anything else? I'm going for a ride." I stand and meet their hardened gazes.

"Nope. We got this," Jagger grumbles.

I slap his back and saunter away from them, trying not to prance all the way back to my bike where I will no doubt eagerly yank out my phone and text back the girl who's always on my mind.

Once I'm straddling my bike, I pull out my phone.

Hali: I know we weren't supposed to go out until tomorrow but I really need to see you.

My cock thickens under my thick denim jeans. We've been on several dates. All of them end with her straddling me in my jeep with her tongue down my throat. I've been dying to fuck her, to claim her as mine, but I'm trying to be a man who deserves her in the first place.

Me: You just miss it when I sniff you.

A grin tugs at my lips. I fire up the engine but don't leave the parking lot. Soon, my phone chimes again.

Hali: Can you come to my place? I need you right now.

Now, I'm going crazy with desire to strip her down and tongue every inch of her body.

Me: Address, beautiful.
Hali: Bring your gun just in case.

All the blood rushing to my cock runs cold. The address pops up on the screen next, and I waste no time tearing off down the road in that direction. If someone tries to hurt her, I'll fucking skin them right in front of her. Nobody touches her. Absolutely no one.

I pull up to a fancy apartment complex that overlooks the ocean. Once I park, I pull my piece from my holster and chamber a bullet. Then, I stalk toward the apartment number she gave me. When I reach the door, I hear shouting inside. My first instinct is to barge right in. Unfortunately, it's locked.

With my fist, I pound on the door. "Open up!"

The shouting, from a male, stops, and I can only hear her sweet sobs from the other side. I'm about to bust open a window when I hear the deadbolt disengage. The moment the door swings open, I shove the barrel of my gun into the chest of a smarmy looking motherfucker.

"You hurt her?" I seethe, venomous rage surging through me.

His eyes dilate and he sways. Drunk ass psycho.

"No, but you will," he snaps and bares his teeth.

My gaze flits to where she sits in the middle of the living room floor. Shards of glass litter the carpet around her and her face is buried in her hands as she cries.

"Step the fuck back," I order.

He grits his teeth but makes his way down the hallway toward the living room.

"Sit on the couch. Keep your hands where I can see them," I hiss. My eyes don't leave his but I reach for Hali. "Come here, beautiful."

She launches to her feet and throws herself into my arms. I snake my free arm around her tiny frame, hugging her to me.

"You're coming with me. Pack a bag. I'll keep you safe."

When she reluctantly peels herself from my body and hurries to the bedroom, I turn my attention back to the weasel.

"Who are you?"

He shrugs his shoulders. "Her boyfriend."

I stiffen at his words and it takes everything in me not to unload my entire magazine into his chest. "Bullshit. You her roommate, Steff?"

His non-response tells me all I need to know. When she mentioned Steff, I assumed it was a chick. Had I known it was a fucking man this entire time, I'd have already whisked her away with me.

"You're not to look at her. To touch her. To fucking talk to her, asshole. You got me?" I snarl. "She's not yours."

He scoffs at my words. "She's not yours either. The little princess is my responsibility. If I find out you're fucking her, I will kill you."

This time, I laugh at his words. "Just try it, punk. Fucking try it."

Hali rounds the corner with a backpack secured on her shoulders. Her hair has been pulled into a messy bun. For once, she's not smiling, and it makes me want to throttle that fucker for making her upset. When I see the red mark on her cheek bone, I go blind with rage.

"Please," she begs, seeing my impending explosion. "Let's just get out of here, Mad."

"DON'T FUCK HER!" Steffan's threat is shouted at us, but it falls on deaf ears as we leave.

With my eyes steady on him, I motion for her to go to the front door. He doesn't follow us out, but my eyes stay on the door even as she straddles the bike behind me. I'm not calm until her arms are wrapped around my middle and we're cruising toward my condo. By the time we reach my place, it's dark.

"Come on," I tell her as we climb off. Her hand finds mine, and I guide her into my dark house. Once inside, I turn on the light and take her backpack from her. "Spill it, beautiful. Did that motherfucker hurt you?"

Tears well in her eyes and she throws herself into my arms. "He's my friend. Truthfully. But we met in the strangest of ways. It was like he was waiting for me. If I didn't know any better, I'd think my father sent him to watch over me. He's crazy possessive, which is mostly why I haven't dated in the two years I've been here. I always give him the benefit of the doubt, but ever since I've started dating you over the past couple of weeks, he's been losing it. I've been careful to hide my phone from him because he's notorious for invading my privacy. It's just become so toxic lately. I don't know what I'm going to do. Maybe once he cools off I can—"

"You're not going back there," I cut her off. "Ever. There's no way that fucker is ever going to touch you again. You can stay here." I slide my fingers into her hair and dip down to kiss her trembling lips. "You can relax here. You're safe."

When she pulls away, her eyes are red from crying. "I think a swim will loosen me up. I'm just emotionally drained and need to take my mind from it all."

I smile at her. "Go put your swimsuit on. I'll grab mine and something to drink. Meet me on the back deck and we'll go down together.

Fifteen minutes later, Hali emerges from the condo, donning the tiniest black bikini I've ever seen. The top barely covers her perky tits. It's nothing but strings and small triangles. Fucking perfect.

Hiding my hard cock behind the bottle of tequila, I motion with my head toward the ocean. "You ready, beautiful?"

She beams at my words and nods. We thread our fingers together, walking hand in hand. Once we are near the water, I drop both towels into the sand and unscrew the tequila. We share a few sips, our eyes never leaving the other, and then I twist the cap back on.

I'm about to motion to the water when she reaches behind her and tugs at the string. The black scrap loosens before the entire top falls into the sand. Her eyes remain focused on her task of getting naked. And my gaze is on her perfect body, visually tasting every single inch of her flesh. Once her bottoms hit the sand too, I watch with pleasure when she runs toward the crashing waves, her creamy white ass bouncing every step of the way.

I don't remember shedding my trunks.

Or the run to the water.

I certainly don't remember diving under the

surf like a shark hungry for his prey.

My only focus is her.

Always her.

chapter four

Hali

"Tell me about work. How was your day?" I question. I'm eager to take his concerned, probing eyes from me. I want to forget tonight even happened. How my only friend here in Miami backhanded me across the face. If my father found out, he'd laugh at me. Tell me I deserved it for making such shit decisions.

He grumbles as he reaches for me. I'm pulled into his warm arms as the waves crash around us. His furry chest tickles my breasts, causing me to shiver. It takes everything in me not to straddle him right now. But dear God, how I want to. His thick erection is sandwiched between our naked bodies.

43

I wonder how it will feel the first time he pushes it into me. Will he split me in two or will my body adjust to take him?

"You don't need to hear about all that bad stuff. You're too sweet," he coos and nuzzles his nose against the side of my neck. I let out a gasp when his lips suckle the flesh right below my ear. This time, my legs do wrap around him. His cock rests against my pussy, and I pray he'll just shove it in.

"I'm not sweet. The thoughts running through my head are far from sweet, Madden. When I'm around you, I can't think straight. My thoughts resemble that of a teenage boy," I say with a laugh.

His teeth bite down, nearly to the point of pain on my neck, but then he tongues the sore flesh there. "Teenage boys don't have this," he breathes against my neck as his hand slips between us. The moment his middle finger slides against my clit, I buck in his arms.

"Oh, God," I moan, tossing my head back.

He chuckles, deep and throaty, which only makes me more needy for him. I'm about to tell him to just fuck me already, when his finger slips between my pussy lips and slowly enters me. His thick digit stretches me, and I grind against his hand. He then digs the heel of his hand against my clit, massaging me in a wicked way that has unearthly noises coming from me.

"Madden—I—what're you—oh, God!"

The stars, so brilliant and bright in the sky, tilt and whirl above me. With every movement of his hand beneath the water, I fall further and further into his vortex. I could die after this moment and feel completely satisfied with my time here on this earth. His teeth find my ear this time, causing me to lose all sense of reality. The sensations are all too much—too perfect. My entire body suddenly convulses as he brings me to a pleasure my own hands have yet to achieve. I shudder for an entire minute before I relax in his arms.

"I want you in ways I can't fully describe or understand, Hali," he murmurs against my ear, his hot breath sending endless shivers down my spine. "Every part of me aches to join with every part of you. You've bewitched me, woman."

I laugh and wiggle in his arms. "Take me in the ways you can understand for now. We'll figure out the rest as we go. We're doing good so far, biker boy."

And at that, he tells me to hang on. Once my arms are wrapped around his neck, he grabs onto my hips and guides me over the tip of his cock. I'm wondering if he'll go fast or slow when he thrusts fully into me, while pulling me down over him. An explosion of pain causes me to cry out. But then his fingers are probing my sensitive clit again, distracting me completely.

"Shhhh, angel," he murmurs as he pumps into me. "You're mine now. Do you like when I'm inside you? Do you feel like you belong to me?"

Our lips meet again and I kiss him deeply. When I moan, I let out the words he's been dying to hear. "Yes. So good. You feel so good, Mad."

My eyes close when an orgasm rips through me, even more intense than the time before. I'm completely owned by this bad boy biker. We were meant to meet. He was supposed to see me enter the shop that day. And I was supposed to drool over him every time he came sauntering in, his hungry eyes all over my body. I absolutely believe in fate.

When I come back down from my high, I feel his heat pour into me. I'm too drugged up on Madden Finn to consider the repercussions or consequences. Instead, I snuggle closer to him and enjoy the way his strong arms hold me tight against him. I feel him soften inside me, and with it, his semen runs out to mix in the ocean water.

"I kind of lost control there," he says in a whisper. "It felt right though. I didn't want to stop."

I pull away to regard his dark eyes. "Are we weird? Do normal people feel this way after sex with someone they really like?"

He smirks at me. "You're weird. I'm a badass."

Laughing, I shake my head at him. "You got that backwards, biker boy. I'm the badass and you're the weirdo."

When our laughter dies down, he regards me with a serious expression. "I don't think this is normal. It feels unlike anything I've ever experienced. I've been around the block a few damn times, and I certainly have never fucked a woman without a condom on."

I run my palm up his sculpted chest to his neck. "And I've never had sex. Seems like we're doing all sorts of crazy things together. Perhaps we're bad for each other."

He growls and kisses me again. His cock hardens within me. I'm not sure if I'll enjoy another round this soon, but I'll be damned if I don't try.

"I like being bad with you," he tells me in a conspiratorial tone.

I giggle against his lips. "I like being bad with you too."

"I like your shower," I tell him as I emerge from the bathroom in just a towel.

His eyes roam my body before he grins crookedly at me. "I like you naked in my shower. And now, I want you naked in my bed."

I drop the towel and eat up the ravenous way he looks over my body. Twice, earlier in the ocean, was probably one too many times for my sore body, but I'm already growing wet beneath his gaze.

We crawl into bed and he pulls me to him. His giant arm wraps around my middle and cups my breast. My heart rate quickens at feeling his thick, erect cock between the cheeks of my ass. Luckily, he remains still. As much as I want him again, I'm unsure I can take it.

"I like you here, sea angel."

Giggling, I cover his hand with mine. "Sea angel? I thought we determined I was bad, right along with you."

His hearty chuckle warms my heart. "You're bad, no denying that. But it's the good kind of bad. The kind of bad that makes a grown man crazy. Besides, tonight, in the ocean under the moonlight, you were ethereal. I swear, I was making love to an angel. So now you're my sea angel."

I close my eyes, reveling in his words. Is this what people search for their entire lives? I've never felt so complete and wanted. My heart throbs to life whenever I look at him. This has to be what everyone's always gabbing about. And I want to gab about it, too. Right here from this bed. Because I'm never leaving.

"Tell me about Steffan," he says softly, a bite of anger in his voice.

I stiffen in his arms. My words still on my tongue for a moment. Eventually, I find my voice. "He's rough around the edges. Protective—overly so. I'm not even sure what he does for a living. He tells me it's illegal and that's enough probing for me. If he didn't find me when I was at my lowest, there would be no loyalty to him. But he did find me. And it breaks my heart it's come down to this."

"So he's jealous?"

I bite my bottom lip and nod. "He's always envisioned a relationship between us that goes beyond friendship. For me, I just don't feel it when I'm around him. I'm thankful for him and sometimes he can be funny. And he always looks after me. But he doesn't make it hard to breathe like you do. He doesn't seem to ignite my entire body with flames, but you do. Everything's just different with you."

His thumb runs over my nipple, making it harden at his touch. "Have you ever just wanted to run away from it all?"

I freeze at his words. "Yes."

"And what did you do?"

"I ran away from it all." My words come out clipped and cold. Images of my father and Zee flash in my mind. I force them from my head. They're not here.

"Hey," he coos against my neck, "it brought you here."

Relaxing, I nod. "That it did."

"What anchors you here?"

I consider his words. At one time, Steffan. I'm loyal, but he crushed that loyalty once and for all when he put his hands on me. My job at the froyo stand is temporary, just something to bring in cash to support my photography. And then there's Madden.

"Just you right now."

"So would you ever go away? You know, if things between us worked out? Could you just leave this all behind and start over?" he questions.

Hope is laced with his words.

Unsure. Unsteady. Uneasy.

But, hope is there.

"I think I could. But could you?"

His teeth nip at the flesh on my shoulder. "I would go anywhere with you."

"You're drunk," I say with a giggle.

"Drunk on you."

I let out a full-bellied laugh, to which he begins tickling me. It's a flurry of kicks and screams until he has me pinned beneath him. My chest heaves, but our eyes are glued to one another.

"My craving for you gets more and more intense. I can't quit you, Hali."

Freeing my legs, I then wrap them around his waist. I want him inside of me. I want to feel the painful burn of his body inside of mine. The addiction is there for me too.

"So don't quit, Madden Finn. Please, don't ever quit."

We've spent four blissful weeks in our bubble. I quit Franny's and spend every waking moment in Madden's arms. He makes less and less frequent trips to the clubhouse, to the point I'm beginning to worry they'll be angry with him. Steffan, surprisingly so, hasn't tried to communicate with me at all. Like I said, bliss.

But today, Madden's not his usual self.

"Everything okay?" I question as I lick the spoon I've been stirring the spaghetti with.

He leans his hip against the counter and runs his fingers through his disheveled hair. Today, he's hotter than ever in a pair of low-slung faded and holey jeans, with no shirt on. Each curve of his muscular chest begs to be licked. Instead, I settle for running my tongue along my upper lip. His eyes narrow on my mouth before he speaks, lines of worry etching his handsome face. "No, it isn't actually."

Quivers of uncertainty shake their way through me. I force a smile. Have I done something wrong to piss him off? Is he tired of me? Am I not a good enough lover? "What's wrong, Mad?"

"I want to leave this place. Together. You and I can start someplace new where nobody knows our names." His voice is gruff, but I sense pain in his words.

"That sounds wonderful," I say with an encouraging smile.

"But…"

My heart thunders in my chest. "That doesn't sound good."

"We can't go into this with secrets. I've told you mine. All but one," he says gruffly. "But I want to."

I can't help but think about my own past. We never broach the subject much, of my father, but if he tells me what's bothering him, he's going to expect the same of me. When I left two years ago, I vowed to bury that part of myself. To burn away the memory and pretend it doesn't exist.

"You don't have to tell me. We're fine. We'll be fine," I blurt out as I turn the stove off.

His worried eyes have darkened. I see them assessing me, seeking out answers I'm unwilling to give. "We won't be fine. This is a part of who I am. You need to understand this part about me and if you choose to leave me—"

"I won't ever leave you," I vow, my brows furled together.

He scoffs. "Don't make that promise yet, beautiful."

An hour later and we're both walking silently hand in hand toward the beach. Because the beach is so secluded, we don't even bother with clothes anymore for the walk to the ocean, since we're going to strip down when we get there anyway. When we reach the water's edge, he tugs his hand from mine and storms toward the waves. His complexion has gotten tanner since he spends so much time out here with me, and I stare at his golden sculpted ass until he dives under the surf.

With a nervous sigh, I splash out after him. Once we're both deep enough we have to tread water, I dip under the water and wet my hair. When I come back up, he's regarding me with a scowl. For a brief moment, I have a panic attack. What did he see? One glance around me, tells me I have nothing to fear. Everything is normal.

His arms wrap around me and he tugs me to him. Our lips connect for a hurried, hungry kiss before he pushes away just a little. Water rivulets run down his temples, his dark hair hangs down past his brows, and his lips are pulled into a frown. Whatever it is that's upsetting him is upsetting me too. I'm on the verge of tears.

"So you know I'm adopted right?

Chewing on my bottom lip, I nod.

"I don't know where I came from or anything. My adopted mother says there isn't much to know, just that she took care of me. Truth is, I don't think she legally adopted me. You see…"

"Yes?"

He kisses me once more, as if I might disappear simply from him thinking about what it is he wants to tell me. Surely, it can't be that bad, can it?

"I don't think I'm human." His voice is sad, bitter even.

The breath is sucked right from my chest. "I, uh…"

"Just listen. I'm different. I'd like to show you, but swear to God you won't freak the fuck out, Hali. I need you," he begs. "Promise me."

I swallow the thick ball of emotion in my throat. "Promise."

Another kiss.

"I'm going to show you. It's easier that way."

Tears are welling in my eyes. My heart is expanding more and more with each passing second, until it might explode. This cannot be true. This cannot fucking be true.

"Stay there," he instructs.

All I can do is stare at him. With a nervous laugh, he sinks into the water, disappearing once again into the dark depths. My heart continues its wicked stretching and growing. It hurts, but it's a beautiful sort of pain.

The water around me moves forcefully. And when something smooth touches my calf, I let out a surprised gasp. I know that smoothness. I've felt it before. It's familiar.

My heart rate quickens when he doesn't re-emerge. Deep down, I know. I understand. But I need confirmation. After several minutes, his head resurfaces. The dark hair hangs in his eyes as he takes a breath. Our eyes meet, and I shiver. Gone are his almost black eyes. Now, they shimmer a radiant midnight blue. His skin seems almost translucent in the sunlight.

His smile, though.

His smile is more brilliant than the sun on the hottest day.

He's absolutely beautiful.

"Are you scared?" he murmurs, his low voice almost musical in quality.

When I shake my head no, his grin widens.

"Good. Now let me show you the best part."

He dips back under the water. A moment later, a large tail of the aquatic variety thrashes the water in front of me, splashing my face. The tail is sparkly and that same midnight blue of his eyes. It's absolutely breathtaking.

Tears well in my eyes, and I let out a sob.

My heart finally bursts, no longer content with exponential growing.

Time to face the facts.

My boyfriend is a merman.

chapter five

Madden

I'M HIDING BENEATH THE SURFACE AGAIN. I'D seen the understanding in her eyes. The utter acceptance. But what if I'd been wrong. What if I fucked up completely? Would she swim back to the beach and keep on running?

Frustrated with myself, I dive deep toward the ocean floor. Once I'm satisfied I'm far enough away from her, I skim my palms along the sandy bottom in search of another shell. I want to find all of them for her. To line them up on my back deck so she can photograph them all. And then, I'll make wind chimes out of them for my adopted mother.

I'm startled when something flits along my tail.

Jerking around to face my attacker, I'm shocked when I find myself staring into two dazzling emeralds that dance with mischief. A sea of shining reddish blonde floats around the most beautiful face I've ever seen.

I blink at her in surprise. She's different. Somehow even prettier down here below the surface. When she smiles, her white teeth nearly blind me.

"Hali…" My words trail off because I then notice the rest of her. All of her. The sheer perfection. A mermaid.

"Apparently we share the same secret," she says in a singsong voice. The sound is decadent and addicting. I've never heard a sound like it before. I'm completely mesmerized by her.

"This is incredible. I don't understand. How?"

She slides her arms around my neck and pulls herself to me. Her full breasts press against my chest and my entire body rages with need. I'm almost blinded by the urge to mark her. To make her mine for the whole goddamn ocean to see.

"I come from an entire family of mer people back in Cape Town. In South Africa, there's an entire colony of us. We inhabit most of the west side," she tells me, her eyes eyeing my lips as if she's starved for them. "But I left them. My family is overbearing. Suffocating even. Father wanted me to marry Zee. It's all political and not my style. I wanted to find love, not be forced into an unhappy marriage."

I slip my palm to her cheek and stroke her unbelievably soft flesh. She's so much more breathtaking in mermaid form. Her skin is perfection, her hair lush, her green eyes beautiful, her voice the most amazing fucking song. And her tail. Her goddamn tail is a thing too unique for this world.

"I can't believe there are more like me," I tell her. My lips find hers and our kiss is an all body event. I can sense her infecting every part of me in a delicious way. Every part of me craves to intertwine with her.

"Many," she assures me. "This is like a dream come true, Madden. You're perfect for me."

I hug her to me. My chest begins to ache and we'll need to resurface soon. Just because I'm a merman, it doesn't mean I can breathe forever underwater. It just means I can breathe for several minutes. Holding her tight, I swish my tail and surge us to the top. Once we both reemerge, our lips are back on one another. Our tails continuously move, but it's more of a sway and they're in sync with one another, keeping us afloat.

This kiss is so different. Kissing her in mer form is a thousand times better than kissing her on dry land. My entire body thrums and pulsates with satisfaction.

"Hali," I tell her when I reluctantly pull away from her sweet lips. "You're my sea angel. My little mermaid. How fucking cute are you? God, I love you."

Her lips break into a full grin. "I love you too, Mad."

I'm about to kiss her again when I hear the familiar squeaking of a dolphin. Sometimes on my swims, they find me and swim alongside. I can't communicate with them, but they somehow seem to understand me. Another one joins the first and they swim circles around us, all the while chattering to one another. They sound excited. Happy even.

"What's this all about?" I question with a laugh.

Hali giggles. "They think we're getting married. When mer people are in love, their connection can be felt for miles. Dolphins are always instrumental in the ceremonies. A marriage doesn't exist without their blessing."

My hand finds her jaw, and I stare into her

glimmering eyes. "If they think it, and are giving us their blessing, then we should do it. Marry me, Hali. Let's do it. I can fucking feel it coursing through me like electricity. Can you feel it too?"

She chews on her bottom lip and nods. "I do feel it. And apparently they do, too."

"Well, holy shit. How do I make you my wife, sea angel?" I demand with a growl as my other palm slides to the swell of her ass I can feel beneath the sleek skin of her tail. I know it's hiding in there.

Her hand reaches out and she strokes the dolphin passing by. "We do what feels right and then it's done. That's how these things go. Marriage between mer is private and special. Each mermaid and merman is different."

I thread my fingers in her hair and kiss her again. Just below my navel where my human skin disappears into my tail, I begin to feel an ache. A goddamn yearning. This overwhelming desire to mate with her.

"Is this okay?" I question as I turn her around in my arms. Her back is pressed against my chest and her round bottom rubs against the front of my tail. The feeling is intense. I immediately crave more of her.

My palms cup her bare breasts and my lips find the side of her neck. I suckle her until she's moaning the most beautiful song. The need to mate becomes a starvation of my soul. I don't know what I'm supposed to do with her, or how I'll have her, but deep down I know it happens here. Not back at my condo. Not on the beach. Not with her long legs wrapped around me. This is something else altogether. Something fucking magical.

"I don't know what to do," I tell her and nip at her flesh near her ear. "I just need to be with you. Completely."

She whimpers and wiggles her bottom at me. It seems to unlock something in my psyche because I feel an erection beneath the slick skin of my tail. This has never happened to me in my mer form before. But I swear to God, it feels like when I get hard. Except this time, it's exhilarating and animalistic. Normally, when I get ready to turn back into my human form, my tail begins splitting from the top, below my naval and also along the crack of my ass, all the way down to where my feet are. A seam forms between both legs along the front and backside of my tail. The skin eventually dissolves and melts away into the ocean, freeing my legs completely. Yet this time, the split happens right where my hard cock seems to be trying to escape and only frees that part of me. When the cool water wraps around my dick, I let out a hiss.

"I think we can make love this way. My body is doing something, Hali."

She nods and lets out a yelp. "Something is happening to me to. I need you," she moans, "here." Her tiny hand wraps around what feels like my cock, only thicker and more sensitive, and guides me to a soft crease along her backside. Like my body, hers seems to be reforming and adjusting to take me. Unsure if it'll hurt her or not, I take my time sliding into her heat.

"Ahhh!" she cries out from pleasure, not pain.

I groan, but still, in an effort not to ruin what we're doing by coming like a fucking teenager. "Shhh," I mutter against her soft flesh. "Let me love you."

My hands worship her tits while I slowly thrust against her. The sensations are intense. Several times, I nearly black out from the intense surges of orgasmic pleasure that are jolting through me.

"Baby, I don't know how to make you feel good this way," I admit with a grunt.

Her arms reach up behind her and she threads her fingers into my hair. "This. What you're doing, right now. This is better than any orgasm you've ever given to me. I feel like I'm going to explode, Madden."

When she grips my hair, almost angrily, I begin pounding against her more forcefully. The dolphins still circle us but have widened their radius, giving us some privacy. My entire body tightens, causing me to pinch her nipples in response.

"I love you," I hiss against the side of her throat, a second before my world turns blissfully white. My orgasm is full body. Heat floods from me, pouring into her, and I feel as though I've drained my soul into her. Every last bit of it. It feels fucking amazing.

She cries out, a sound more beautiful than any song on this earth, before her body quakes in my arms. I feel a tightening around my cock before her body seems to close, pushing me out in the process. We both chuckle upon realizing our first time as mer people is officially over.

"So beautiful, sea angel."

She twists in my arms and smiles at me. "Do you feel it? It's like your hand is wrapped around my heart. Gripping it. Owning it. I'm linked to you,

Mad."

The ache in my chest is from her. It's indescribable. We're tethered by an invisible bond. Too perfect to be seen or touched by anyone. Nobody can sever our bond. Fucking nobody.

"Well look what the goddamned cat dragged in." Jagger's tone is harsh. I don't miss the fact he's sitting in my seat at the head of the table.

"Last I checked, I was above you and that was my chair." My snarl has him grunting and moving to the bench. "Where are we at on Ramone?"

As Jagger starts in, I massage the muscle on the right side of my neck and sit down. It's been three weeks since Hali and I made love in mer form in the ocean for the first time. Now, every waking moment, we're exploring the ocean together. She even conned me into buying her an expensive underwater camera so she could take pictures of the sea life. I can't get enough of her, my wife, and I fuck her just as much when we're out of the water.

"What do you think?" Jagger questions, snatching me right from my blissful thoughts.

And this here is the problem. Life is getting in the fucking way of me possessing every molecule in her body. My responsibilities to this club are becoming a nuisance. I'm not cut out to lead them anymore. Hell, I don't even care if I ever step foot in this clubhouse again. And that's not fair to any of these guys. This club is their life.

My life is Hali.

"Repeat the last part," I say gruffly.

"Guttenberg."

I scowl at him. "Come again?"

"The new guy, the one we've checked out is called, Guttenberg. Some German fuck. Anyway, he's got the goods. Cass and I already inspected his product. All we need is your okay on it, Mad Dog."

My eyes flit to each of the men surrounding the table. I can see it in their expressions. Frustration. Irritation. Disappointment. It only solidifies what I came here to do today. They deserve more.

"Actually, Jagger," I say and run my fingers through my hair, tousling it up. "Club rules state in the event of death of the president, VP steps up in his place."

He stiffens from beside me and frowns. "You

plan on dying soon, mate?"

The room is silent. I'm not sure any of them are breathing, simply holding a collective breath.

"I may as well be dead, huh? I've failed you all as president. My head's gotten all twisted up with something else. It's not fair to keep stringing you all along." I scratch at the scruff on my jawline, another reminder of Hali. She likes it when I'm not clean shaven. Says I'm rugged and shit. "So, as the rules state, if the president dies or must leave his position, vice president takes over. This is my official resignation."

Cassius lets out a full-bellied laugh, and several of the guys laugh nervously with him. "You're shitting me right? What is this, April Fool's or some crap?"

I give him a brief shake of my head. "I'm out, man."

Jagger growls from beside me. Of course, he would be the most upset. We've been close since we were teenagers.

"Is this about a fuckin' chick," Steam demands, his voice dripping with disgust. "Club is full of willing whores and you gotta go out to find some strange. Then what? Fall in fuckin' love like a goddamned pussy?"

"THAT IS ENOUGH!" Jagger roars and slams his fists into the table.

Steam has the sense to look nervous. He should be. Jagger's his boss man now.

"Take care," I say with a grunt as I stand.

"You leave and your money doesn't follow. It's club money. When you quit the Sinners, you don't roll like a saint," Cassius reminds me with sneer.

Jagger shoots him a glare. "What part of I've had a fucking 'nough did you not get, asshole? Nobody moves. I'll be back in five," he barks out, his authority already being felt by the group. "I'll walk you out."

I nod and stand. All eyes are on me as I remove my jacket and toss it on the table. I give Moe a squeeze on his shoulder before I start out. "You guys are like family to me."

"Were," Steam grumbles under his breath.

Jagger growls at him as we pass. Once we're outside, I straddle my bike and regard him with an apologetic stare. "I'm sorry, man."

He smirks, and the kid I met in Chemistry class is suddenly before me. Haven't seen him in a good decade and a half. "You are in fucking love."

I shrug my shoulders in an attempt to feign disinterest. "Just have a new path I need to follow is all. You've got this shit covered. I'll sell the condo and them I'm out of Miami."

"What does Mama Constance think about this?" His voice is low, careful not to let others in on our conversation. We don't talk about his family, and I don't talk about mine. But we both know about the other since we go way back.

"She won't be happy," I tell him with a grunt. A grin tugs one side of my lips up. "But one look at my girl and she'll give me her blessing. I wish I could elaborate, man. Just trust she's worth leaving my brothers for."

His face darkens, and I swear I sense understanding from him. He nods. "Take care, buddy. Club still has your back. You may be retiring like an old man, but this club has a fucking amazing retirement plan. It's one that involves bullets should the need arise, but a plan that protects you, nonetheless. Always a Sinner, Mad Dog."

He leaves without another word.

I leave a home that has welcomed me over the past decade to move on to my new home—a home that has nothing to do with a roof over my head, but everything to do with a door to my heart.

When I roll up to the condo, I want to climb off my bike and skip like a girl back to Hali. Unfortunately, she's nowhere to be found inside. With a grin, I start chucking clothes as I make my way to the water. Most days, I find her scouring the shallow ends searching for shells. She never strays far, so she can hear me when I call for her.

Once I hit the water, I dive in. Not wasting a second, I transform quickly. As soon as my legs bind together and the ache in my chest subsides, I thrash my tail and dive deep into the water. I call out for her, searching the blue waters for her reddish halo. A smile plays on my lips, as I half expect her to sneak up on me from behind.

But she doesn't.

And I call and call for her.

My pulse spikes as I consider something could be wrong. She never strays from the shore. Where the fuck is she? I'm working myself into a panic when something shiny catches my eye. Her camera. The lens on the front is cracked and the thing just sits on the ocean floor as if it belongs there. I swipe it into my hands. Opening the picture history, I take a look at the last picture she took.

My entire world implodes.

Blackish eyes stare back at me, partially hidden behind her mad sea of reddish blonde hair as I look at the screen. A man, or should I say a fucking *merman*, has a hand clasped over her mouth in the picture. Someone else took the pictures, which means there could be two of them.

What. The. Fuck.

Rage consumes me. I will find those fuckers who took her and I will gut them, flay them, and make fucking fish tacos out of them.

Someone took my heart.

And I won't stop until I have her back.

chapter six

Hali

"WAKE UP, PRINCESS," A COLD, FAMILIAR voice whispers.

My eyelids feel like they've been weighted down, but I attempt to blink them open. "What have you done?" I demand in a shaky voice.

When my eyes focus, I find the nearly black ones of Zee. A shudder ripples through me. My father just couldn't stand it. He had to send in troops.

"I came to fetch what was rightfully mine. Steff said you were getting too close with some guy. Your father told me you needed a vacation. Time to sort things out. We never dreamed you'd run off and try to fuck the first guy you see," he snarls.

I sit up and realize I'm on a hotel bed. The sliding glass door that overlooks the ocean is open. I momentarily contemplate making a run for it when I see the glow of a cigarette in the darkness. Then, in steps Steffan.

"You were in on this?" I question, betrayal making my voice quiver. "You weren't random were you?"

Steffan shrugs his shoulders and laughs. It's dark and fucked up. "No, princess, I was not some random. Such a silly girl. Not street smart at all. Which is why you belong with your goddamned family back at Cape Town where they can keep you from doing stupid shit."

Tears prickle at my eyes, but I refuse to cry. Madden will find me. He has resources. He'd never let these assholes get away with taking me.

"You can't force me to go back there," I tell them both, my tone indignant. "I'll just run away again."

Zee shakes his head and sits beside me. His jaw clenches in a furious way. "You're supposed to wed me, dear girl. This shit was supposed to happen when you turned eighteen. I have been lenient, but I'm tired of waiting. It's been written in the books. Our families have an agreement bound in blood."

I roll my eyes. "We're part human too, mo-ron. You act like we live these magical lives under the ocean, and that I'm supposed to follow bullshit rules that have been around for centuries. Well, newsflash, I don't fucking care. Your father is nothing more than a real estate developer and my dad a damn politician. If the world knew you moonlighted as mermen, you'd be laughed at. Scorned. Times have changed, Zee. The time for arranged marriages and fixed bloodlines is archaic. This royal crap doesn't exist on dry land. I refuse to be a part of it!"

Zee's strong hand is at my throat in an instant. He grips it tightly, but doesn't fully cut off my air supply. In the water, he has monstrous strength. Above water, he's just an asshole.

"Hayden says we're not to hurt her," Steffan says with a growl behind Zee.

A flicker of disappointment flashes in Zee's eyes, but he removes his hand. "Once we're married, you'll learn your place as my wife."

At his words, I hide my hands between my thighs under the blanket that's covering me. I'm wrapped in a robe. It irritates me that they both saw me naked. At the mention of the word wife, my ring finger tingles. I don't need to see my finger to know the pale band, branded in my flesh, is shimmering. It freaked Madden out, once he realized our marriage was permanently etched on his finger. But the first time it glowed while we made love in his dark bedroom after our wedding, he told me it was incredible and beautiful. Like me. A smile plays at my lips.

"What's with the smile, princess?" Zee demands.

Another cold shudder ripples through me, chasing off the warm memory of my husband. "Just thinking about how much I hate you. How I'll run away the first chance I get. Madden will find me and together we'll hide from the likes of you people."

Steffan laughs. "Oh, your biker asshole boyfriend? Looks like you won't have to worry about him too much longer. We're going to take care of him."

"Who are you?" I demand. "Where is the guy who was my friend for two years?"

His glare becomes murderous. "I was always meant to watch you. To keep you pure and virginal for your husband."

"Oh, what a fucking lie, Steff," I bark out. "Did you tell Zee here you tried to fuck me every chance you got?"

Zee snaps his gaze to Steff. "What the hell is she going on about?"

Steffan has the sense to look afraid. He should be. Zee is not one to fuck around with. My father is the most powerful and revered in our family. Zee, after his father died suddenly and rather questionably, became the most powerful man in his. Steffan is nothing more than a commoner with our kind. A damn minion.

"She's lying. I didn't touch her."

I shrug my shoulders. "Whatever. I want to talk to my dad."

Zee laughs and shakes his head. "You sure you're ready for his wrath, princess? The old man took the first flight he could, once I told him we had you. He's ready to give you an old fashioned ass whipping. And then you're mine."

My eyes skim the room, and I once again wonder if I'd be quick enough to slip out the door without them catching me. "I don't belong to any of you."

Zee is about to argue when someone pounds on the door. My heart thunders in my chest, hoping Madden has found me. But when Steffan opens the door, my world crashes down around me.

Hayden Morgan.

All six foot seven inches and shoulders that would match any linebacker.

My father, with his dark red hair and emerald orbs, eyes me with a venomous glare.

"Your royal highness," Steffan says in awe, before falling to one knee. "Or, uh, King. I'm not really sure what to call you."

I want to drag him back to his feet by his hair. Apparently, Father feels the same way because he does just that.

"Dear God. You call me Hayden. What a dreadful piece of trash you are. I can't believe you've been responsible for her safety this entire time. It's a title, urchin, not a fucking order for you to bow like a goddamned peasant. This doesn't work on dry land, Steffan Guttenberg. Don't ever do that again, or I'll have Zee kill you before you take your next breath."

Dear old Dad's here.

And he wonders why I left.

"Find my daughter some clothes, urchin," Father barks to Steffan. "It's time we go back to Cape Town and settle this affair by tomorrow. You exhaust me, dear daughter."

Zee laughs, and I crave to take away any shred

of happiness. So, I do just that.

"Actually, I'm already married, Father."

The room goes silent as Zee and my father exchange a look.

"That's nonsense. Now, you'll dress and—" my father starts, but I interrupt him by waving my hand in the air.

"I. Am. Married. To. Madden Finn." The light catches the sparkly band and it glimmers.

Zee's eyes widen as he stalks over to me, snatching my hand to take a better look. "This is impossible. You can't have married another man. Tell her this is a fraud, Hayden."

But my father is gaping at me in horror. "A mer?"

Tears well in my eyes, and I nod. "We had a proper ceremony between two mer people. The dolphins were even fucking there!" My voice rises a few octaves. "I'm happily married too, so if you'll excuse me, I'll be leaving, motherfuckers!"

"Don't take that tone with me, young lady," Father thunders, his freckly face turning bright red with fury. "You're not going anywhere until we sort out what you've started, goddammit!"

My laugh is crazed. "You can't undo shit, Father. It's done. It's legal among our kind and binding. You know that better than anyone. Our souls are intertwined."

Zee grabs a handful of my hair and hauls me to my knees. I flash my teary gaze to my father, who offers no help. Just an irritated scowl.

"It can be undone, princess. And Steffan will make sure of it," Zee threatens.

"How?" I shriek. I can't imagine the bond breaking between Mad and I. In fact, it seems to grow more and more each day. It's impossible. "You're lying."

Father shrugs his shoulders. "The bond will break when either husband or wife dies."

I start to scream and claw at Zee. But he easily wrangles me to the bed, while Steffan handcuffs my wrist. Once it's secured to the bed frame, they both step away. I continue to thrash, spitting out every profanity in the book.

"You will all pay for this!" I screech.

"No, actually your dear fraudulent husband is about to pay," Steffan sneers. "With his life."

With that statement, I burst into tears.

mad sea

"Little cherub of the sea, come and play with me.

Come and play with me, dearest cherub of the sea.

Please come play with me,

In the mad, mad sea."

My dream calms me, and I try to hold on to the memory of that voice. During childbirth, while delivering me, my mother died. It was her best friend Malena who saw to it I was properly nursed. Malena employed her governess, Mrs. Finley, to do the job. Mrs. Finley was already a nursemaid who cared for Malena's own small boy, and then her child on the way. This woman had recently lost a baby of her own and continued to produce milk of which I benefited from. I don't have many memories of Mrs. Finley. Just the lingering song that replays in my head. She disappeared and nobody talks about what happened.

"Little cherub of the sea." The soft voice feels real this time. My heart clenches.

I flutter my eyes open and stare into the pretties

blue eyes I've ever seen. "Is this a dream?"

The woman, with the mane of blonde hair and a kind face, smiles. "No, child. Do you remember me?"

I furrow my brows together. "I know your voice. Are you Mrs. Finley?"

Tears well in her eyes, and she nods. "So you do remember, love. That, I am. Sit tight, dear girl, I'm going to get you out of here."

She climbs off the bed and retrieves a bag from the floor. I gape in surprise when she pulls out a hand saw. Then, she sets to cutting away at the wooden bed frame I'm attached to. When I break free, handcuff still attached to my wrist, she hugs me.

"How did you know I was here?" I question as she strokes my hair. Mrs. Finley smells like sunshine and lemonade. Her hug warms me, much like my mother's would have if she would have lived, and I take comfort from it.

She pulls away and regards me seriously. "Long ago, I left our people. Once I saw what Malena's husband, Zute, had done to her, I couldn't bear to stay and witness any more corruption. Zute strangled that poor woman. They were discussing the fate of their lineage. Malena feared the communityty would hate her eldest son, Zadden, since he'd not had the change yet. Most mer change around their first birthday. But at six, he still hadn't changed. The boy was to inherit their fortune and was destined to marry you. As soon as they realized he was seemingly defective, they worked hard to produce another son. When Zee was born and changed at just eight months old, Zute told Malena they must eliminate their first child. She begged him not to and that's when he strangled her. I'd slipped out with Zadden. I stole that sweet boy and raised him as my own here in America."

Mrs. Finley helps me out of the bed and together we slip out the sliding glass door. There's a jeep outside waiting with the engine running. Once we're on the road, she takes my hand and flashes me a smile.

"You saved him, Mrs. Finley," I say. "Our people can be cruel."

She nods, hitting the accelerator. "That, they can be. And please, call me Constance."

Jerking my head in her direction, I gape at her. "Constance Finn? You're…"

Her laughter is like ringing bells in a church—

powerful, warm, inviting. "Yes, I'm Madden's adopted mother."

My belly flops as tears well in my eyes. "My Mad is, Zadden, Zee's older brother?"

"He is, darling. And now we must get you someplace safe."

"How did you find me?" I question again. Nothing makes any sense, but I can't help but feel like fate's plan was never derailed, despite anyone's meddling.

"Let's just say the dolphins around here are quite the gossip," she says with a mischievous wink. "Well, that and I've had eyes on Zute ever since I took Madden all those years ago. My cousin, Arda, is on Zute's payroll. She sends me everything pertaining to that family, and yours. Hotels, flight numbers, itineraries."

I chew on my bottom lip as I attempt to digest everything. "Does Madden know?"

"Don't you worry about my boy, Hali. He's always been able to roll with the punches."

"They went to kill him," I choke out, tears spilling out over my cheeks. "How could my father do that to me?"

Constance laughs. "I can assure you, those suits

and that bottom feeder have nothing. Absolutely nothing on my son. He was destined to become King. In fact, rightfully so, he *is* King after your marriage to him. And a king is not weak. Not weak at all."

I close my eyes and think about how powerful he is, whether it be with a hog between his muscular thighs, or how his massive tail sluices through the water as he swims at breakneck speeds, or even how he looked like a giant sitting in the green plastic chair at Franny's. There's nothing weak about my husband at all.

My king.

Take that, dear 'ol Dad.

chapter seven

Madden

"ONE LAST RUN FOR OLD TIME'S SAKE?" Jagger questions and holds out his fist.

I nod at him, knocking his fist with mine, and then Cassius's before roaring my engine. Then, I set off riding behind Jagger toward the factory for the meet-up. Guttenberg. Some German asshole who thinks he's going to swoop in and steal business in the middle of a presidency change. I can smell stank from a mile away. And everything about this stinks.

"Be alert," I bark out to Jagger, despite my position as president no longer existing. This goes beyond hierarchy, but instead is about brotherhood. Jagger and I may not always see eye to eye or talk much about our pasts. But we have history. On my sixteenth birthday, we went swimming after several beers we'd stolen from his parents' house. It was then, I changed for the first time. Out of fucking nowhere, and completely by surprise, my legs bound together and reformed into a black tail. A fucking merman. Jagger saw. How could he not? He saw every horrifying bit of it. Neither of us spoke about it afterwards, though. Not once did he say a word about it, and our friendship carried on as if it never happened. But it *did* happen. I didn't even tell Mama Constance. It became *my* secret. And apparently Jagger's too, because he never once told.

"Ten 'o clock," Cassius growls.

It's just the three of us on this run. Nobody else needs to see this shit go down. This is more than a business relationship changing hands. This shit is personal. My eyes flit to where he saw movement. Two well-dressed men stand beside a nondescript black vehicle, staring at us as we approach. But the one standing beside them aiming a Glock at us, is the one I want to throttle.

"Guttenberg," I shout out, my fists clenching. "Steffan Guttenberg."

He laughs coldly, and I stop about twenty feet

from him. "And your friends led you right to me. I played them all so easily with this 'deal.' Now you're going to die, asshole."

Smirking, I cut my eyes to Jagger, and then to Cassius. I know where my loyalty lies. "What do you want?"

I hear the crunch of gravel as the two men approach. Both of my boys are tense beside me. One false move and there'll be a bloodbath. The older one, with dark reddish hair, glowers at me.

"You stole her from us," he practically spits out at me.

I raise a brow at him. "Hali does what she wants. You can't stop love, man."

The black-headed younger man growls. "She's supposed to be mine. I'm the rightful heir and she was to be my wife. Then, some fucker swoops in and steals her. This shit ends tonight, and I take her back with me."

At this, I laugh. "Ain't happening, Zee."

His dark eyes widen at the mention of his name. "What the—"

"This is nonsense. Steffan, take care of them."

"What's the matter, Hayden? Can't do your own dirty work? What's the offense of our people if one attempts to murder the king?" I question, my voice calm and collected. "Oh, that's right, death by drowning. Pretty fucking awful way to die for a merman."

Zee and Hayden exchange horrified glances.

"How do you even know about this? This is ridiculous," Hayden barks out and glances nervously at Cassius, who remains as still as a statue, completely unfazed by talk of mer people.

"What? You afraid these boys are going to tell on you? Rat you out to the government or something? Turn you into lab animals?" I ask, shrugging my shoulders. "Nah, these are my brothers. They know everything. A nice dinner at Mama Constance's earlier and everyone is up to speed on all of your bullshit. You will *not* be taking my wife. You will *not* be killing me. And you all *will* fucking take your bow to your new King. Including you, dear brother. Rules are rules in our community."

I give my command with such a thunderous power, all three of them fall to a knee. Hayden's face is so red it looks like it might pop. Zee looks positively disgusted. And Steffan, that psycho, isn't angry at all. He's the one I keep my eye on. Unhinged motherfucker.

K WEBSTER

"You're not Zadden!" Zee bellows. "Zadden was weak!"

Storming over to him, I grab him by his neck and haul him to his feet. I bare my teeth, getting right in his face. "Do you feel the way my hand could crush your windpipe with one squeeze? I'm fucking dying to do it. It's taking all of my strength *not* to kill you. Zadden may not have fit your perfect mold. But, Madden 'Mad Dog' Finn will pull your spine out through your throat and make fucking wind chimes out of your vertebrae to give to his mother," I mutter with a growl. "Not weak at all, brother."

When I hear a hateful roar behind me, I don't have time react and see what the commotion is about before shots ring out in the air. Hayden crawls away, toward the vehicle, as the guns pop off like firecrackers in a bucket. I toss Zee out of the way of the gunfire. With a twist, I yank my pistol from my belt and swing it toward Steffan. But, as quickly as it started, all that's left are echoes in my ears. Cassius and Jagger stand over Steffan's lifeless body with their weapons aimed at him.

"I'm getting too old for this shit," Jagger grumbles and tucks his gun into the back of his jeans.

Cassius slaps his shoulder. "Should I off you now then, fuck face? Go ahead and take my place as prez?"

Jagger shoves him. "Fuck off, Cass. I ain't too old to kill your slimy ass."

Gravel kicks up as Hayden and Zee tear out of the parking lot in their vehicle.

"Run!" I call out after the taillights. "Pussies."

Cassius chuckles from behind me. "You don't fuck with the Southside Sinners. I don't care if you're a goddamned-stupid-ass-wannabe-king mermaid or some shit. Sinners don't play."

I smirk. "Merman, asshole. Mermaids, are the chicks."

"Well, by all means, go get your little mermaid, Mad Dog, and do marital shit. Whatever the hell that is. Cass and I will get rid of the body," Jagger grunts.

Cassius groans. "Fuck that. Call Steam. Fat boy could use the exercise. What's the point of being prez, Jagger, if you don't boss some poor fuckers around and make them do your dirty work?"

Shaking my head, I hold up two fingers in a peace sign. "I'm out. See you on the flip side."

"Pussy-whipped motherfucker!" Cassius calls

out, and then laughs.

I laugh all the way to my bike.

Time to go get my girl.

As soon as the rumble of my bike cuts off, the sound of the chimes fill the air around me. Mama Constance loves those fucking things. And quite frankly, I love them too. The haunted musical sounds tug at memories from my toddler years. A woman, with hair as black as ink, singing to me as she rocked me. I don't have pictures of my birth mother or much to go on, but the wind chimes remind me of her.

When I walk into the house, my adoptive mother is sitting at the bar with her reading glasses at the end of her nose, staring at her laptop.

"Hey Maddy," she says, her eyes still glued to the screen. "Looks like they caught the next flight back to Cape Town. We can all breathe easy again."

I saunter over to her and kiss the top of her head. "They can have their life there. And now that everything is out in the open, I think we'll live ours here."

She smiles and pats my arm. "And your people?"

"My people are here. I think Hali feels the same."

"Good," she says with a sigh. "I want my boy close by. And little Hali's quite a catch, son."

I laugh. "Yes, she is. Speaking of," I question and look up toward the dark windows, "where's my sea angel?"

She waves toward the ocean. "Doing what our people do best. Now, if you won't mind me, I'll be retiring early tonight. This old woman has had enough excitement for a decade. But don't you two dare go anywhere tonight. I want to cook my son and his wife a congratulatory breakfast." She stands and presses a kiss to my cheek. "I'm sorry I sheltered you your entire life. I simply wanted to protect you from them."

"I know, Mom," I tell her. "Thank you for that. I love you, you know?"

Tears well in her eyes. "I do know. I feel it every day. Love you too, Maddy."

Once she's gone, I head outside. I make my way down to the beach. In the moonlight, I see a pale figure swimming out beyond the waves. Hair silky red and blonde, a beautiful mix. I'm desperate to touch her. I start ripping off my clothes as quickly as I can. I've just shoved my boxers down, when two slender wet arms wrap around my middle.

Twisting in her arms, I pull her to me in a tight embrace. "Thank hell you're okay, beautiful. God, I've fucking missed you today."

She giggles and looks up at me. Her green eyes shimmer with love. "I missed you, too. Your mom is awesome. I think I love her."

"She's the best," I say and press a kiss to her lips. "And that's why I've been thinking. Now that everything's out in the open, I thought maybe—"

"Yes. I want to stay here. Close to Constance."

My heart swells, and I tangle my fingers in her wet hair. Our lips crash together as we kiss each other with desperation. She grabs onto my shoulders and practically climbs me like a tree. Sliding a hand to her ass, I help her slide down onto my cock.

"Yes," she moans once she's fully seated on me. "Make love to me."

I stride over to a soft dune of sand. Lying her down on her back, I never lose stride and continue fucking my woman. Her moans are loud enough to wake the neighbors, but thankfully my mom's wind chimes drown out our sounds.

"You're my queen," I tell her.

She smiles against my mouth. "So Constance tells me. Guess now you should worship me."

With a growl, I nip at her ear and then her neck. Her fingernails dig into my shoulders as I pound into her. My body never seems to be close enough to her. Or deep enough. Or our physical union, long enough. I'd die happy, if it meant I could stay like this with her forever.

"Madden!" she gasps when my fingers find her clit.

I massage her until she's careening off the figurative cliff. Her pussy clenches around my cock, and then I'm a goner. She and I are all that remains—the world has become nothing but a blur around us, as I fuck my climax into her. She's slippery and tight and hot as hell. Fucking heaven, this woman.

"We're going to be poor," I tell her with a laugh. "I can't ever see myself being able to part from you long enough to hold down any respectable job."

She grins. "We'll figure it out. We've done a pretty damn good job at it so far."

I pull out of her and then scoop her sandy ass against my chest. With her squealing in my arms, I charge for the ocean. We're not done yet. I think I just saw a couple of voyeuristic dolphins. And we all know what that means…

epilogue

Hali

A year and a half later...

"**H**ALI!!!!"

Madden's horrified yell from upstairs has me hurrying to the front door. Becky, my store helper, already went home for the night so I flip the sign to closed, throw the deadbolt, and then charge toward where he's still screaming my name. My heart thunders in my chest with worry that something's happened. With each step toward our apartment above our store, my blood seems to grow colder and colder.

I push through the door and head straight for

the bathroom.

"Mad," I shriek, "is Lene okay?"

The first thing I notice upon entering the bathroom is there's water everywhere. My eyes flicker over to my baby with the greenest eyes you ever did see and wild black curls. She flashes me a toothy grin. "Momma!"

Madden, bless his heart, is soaked. His black Metallica T-shirt sticks to his muscled torso, and I bite my lip to suppress the urge to attack him. Pregnancy makes me super horny we've learned. And this tiny baby, already growing in my belly, is no different than the last one. I jump him every chance I get.

"What's going on—oh!"

Lene makes a splash. With her tail. "Fish!"

My eyes meet Madden's freaked out ones. Our baby has changed for the first time. Her pudgy little legs are now hidden beneath a cute sparkly green tail.

"Fish!"—splash—"Fish!"—splash—"Fish!" Her giggles are too cute.

I lean over the tub and ruffle her curls. "That's right, baby. You're a mermaid. Can you say mermaid?"

"Mer-may!"

"That's right!"

"And so it begins," Madden say, stress straining his voice. "What if people find out? How will we protect her? If someone tries to take her, so help me I'll put a bullet in their goddamn sk—"

"We'll protect her. Stop your fussing. Finish cleaning up downstairs and I'll take care of it from here," I instruct.

All I get is a growl and a pop on my ass before he leaves.

Several hours later, after Lene has gone to bed, I sit in Madden's lap on the back patio. The sliding glass door is open so we can listen for our daughter. Tonight, the sky is clear and the ocean is rather calm. I inhale the salty sea air before sipping my steamy cup of honey tea.

"Should we close the Pink Pelican? Move far away?" His hand grips my thigh and his entire body is tense.

I couldn't imagine closing our shop and moving elsewhere. My postcards and the wind chimes are popular at the gift shop, but it's the frozen yogurt that allows us to pay the bills. This is our life. Our home. We'd be lost someplace else.

"There are people everywhere, biker boy. We can't run, nor should we. We'll just have to teach her that she can't go changing whenever she wants to. Nothing is going to happen to her. Besides, I thought you liked it here, Mr. Froyo."

He grunts, which makes me chuckle.

"The frozen yogurt is *your* thing, not mine. I sell those wind chimes I make with Mom," he tells me in a deep tone, as if to make himself sound manlier than he already is. "So technically, *you're* the froyo girl."

I laugh. "No way. I'm not the one who goes through a gallon of the pink stuff all by himself every week. You're totally Mr. Froyo."

"Yeah, yeah," he finally admits and clinks his bottle to my mug. "Just don't tell the boys."

Lying my head on his shoulder, I then lean forward and kiss his solid neck. "I don't think Cass has any room to talk. He let Lene stick bows in his hair last time he came over. I think you're good."

"Well Jagger would give me shit."

At this, I burst into a fit of giggles. "As I recall, Jagger has a Pink Pelican punch card. In fact, I think he comes in solely to see Becky. Hmmm," I say with a smile and run my tongue along the flesh near his ear. "Sounds really familiar."

He groans, and I can tell he's growing hard beneath me. So, I set my mug down and straddle him. His eyes twinkle in the moonlight with love and contentment. It's such a beautiful sight. A sight I'll never tire of seeing.

"Ready to show me what a badass you are, Mr. Froyo?" I purr as I grind against his cock that's trying desperately to escape his board shorts.

He sets his beer down and then stands up with me in his arms. His full lips quirk up into a smug grin. "You just want me to lick you like I lick that spoon every day. You're jealous."

"Maybe I am," I admit with a wicked grin. "But I want you to lick me better."

His hands clutch my ass and he gives me a smoldering look. "You've always been my favorite treat, sea angel."

The next few minutes are a flurry of our clothes being torn off and then his ravenous licking and sucking. And he *does* lick me better than that damn spoon. As soon as I'm coming all over his expert tongue, he flips me over onto my elbows and drives his cock deep into me.

We fit so well together.

Man and woman.

Father and mother.

Husband and wife.

Merman and mermaid.

King and Queen.

As he thrusts into me from behind, his hands find mine and he wraps them over the top of my hands. In the darkness, our wedding rings shimmer and glow.

Life always has a plan. You may think you can run from it. Outsmart it. Outplay it. But in the end, it's going to find you.

And it'll be the best thing that's ever happened to you.

the end.

acknowledgements

Thank you to my husband, Matt. You dry my tears when I'm frustrated, encourage me when I'm feeling low, and make me coffee when I turn into a zombie. You're a keeper, my dear. Love you!

A huge thanks to Nikki McCrae. I appreciate everything you do for me. Your reminders and encouragement keep me going and on task. You're a great friend!

Thank you to Sunny Borek. I can't thank you enough for hanging in there when things get weird. Luckily we can be weird together. Thank you, friend!

A huge thanks to Elizabeth Clinton. Thank you for reading EVERYTHING and I mean EVERYTHING I write. You're always so accommodating and quick when I need a pair of eyes on my latest project. Definitely the biggest cheerleader I know! You are a star and I'm proud to have you as a friend!

I want to thank the people who either beta read this book or proofed it early. Nikki McCrae, Elizabeth Clinton, Ella Stewart, Jessica Hollyfield, Amy Bosica, Shannon Martin, Brooklyn Miller, Robin Martin, Amy Simms, Janie Hambic Bostic, Paige Jennifer, Robyn Crawford, and Sunny Borek, (I hope I didn't forget anyone) you all gave me great feedback and the support I needed to carry on. You all give me helpful ideas to make my stories better and give me incredible encouragement. I appreciate all of your comments and suggestions.

A big thank you to my author friends who have given me your friendship and your support. You have no idea how much that means to me.

Thank you to all of my blogger friends both big and small that go above and beyond to always share my stuff. You all rock! #AllBlogsMatter

I'm especially thankful for my Krazy for K Webster's Books reader group. You ladies are wonderful with your support and friendship. Each and every single one of you is amazingly supportive and caring. I love that we can all be weird page sniffers together.

I am totally thankful for my author group, the COPA gals, for being there when I need to take a load off and whine. Y'all rock!

Manda Lee, thank you for loving my little story and fixing it up nice and pretty just like it deserved. A big thank you to Jessica D. Your eyes and support on this project were the extra shine it needed. Love you ladies!

Thank you Stacey Blake for making mer-magic and making this project a beauty! Love you!

A big thanks to my PR gal, Nicole Blanchard. You are fabulous at what you do and keep me on track!

Lastly but certainly not least of all, thank you to all of the wonderful readers out there that are willing to hear my story and enjoy my characters like I do. It means the world to me!

about the author

K Webster is the author of dozens of romance books in many different genres including contemporary romance, historical romance, paranormal romance, dark romance, romantic suspense, and erotic romance. When not spending time with her husband of thirteen years and two adorable children, she's active on social media connecting with her readers.

Her other passions besides writing include reading and graphic design. K can always be found in front of her computer chasing her next idea and taking action. She looks forward to the day when she will see one of her titles on the big screen.

Join K Webster's newsletter to receive a couple of updates a month on new releases and exclusive content.

Alpha & Omega

One smile. One damn beautiful smile infected my heart and soul with such a force that I nearly exploded. All hopes of afterlife and the eagerness to leave this one vanished with that one handsome smile.

Thump.

My heart gave one painful thud and began beating for the first time in its life.

And then he spoke. The beautiful smile had an even more beautiful voice. And with each word, each joke, and, eventually, each touch, I intertwined my soul so intricately with his that I never had a chance of letting go. I fell in love. And suddenly, life wasn't long enough.

***

'Til Death.

***

This is bad. But oh so good. The first kiss we shared was a glimpse into her soul. Her past. Her pain. This kiss is yet another glimpse into her soul. This time, fire and heat. And me.

The thought of her in eternal, torturous agony sends rage swirling in my veins. She can't die. She can't go to Hell. It doesn't make sense. Then a dark thought enters my mind. I'll protect her. Forever.

Please enjoy this excerpt from *Alpha & Omega* which is now available.

Prologue

LIFE IS NOTHING BUT A SEQUENTIAL SERIES OF monotonous repeats. You wake up and then you eat. You work and then you eat. You bathe and then you eat. Oh, and then you sleep.

Over.

And.

Fucking over again.

Life is a blur. Each passing moment is just another second closer to your final destination—six feet under the dirt to be mourned and eventually forgotten.

I wasn't made for life. Unfortunately, I was one of the few who figured out the algorithms of this godforsaken planet and became a slave to the monotony. I knew my ultimate destiny was death.

The overdramatic poet in me craved that end, because maybe then I could actually feel something besides the constant internal clock counting each second until my expiration. My thought was: Let's hurry and get this phase of my existence over with so that I can move the fuck on. Life is like the lobby of a doctor's office. Or waiting to get your driver's license renewed at the DMV.

Boring.

As.

Fuck.

Each day, I toyed with the idea of speeding the process up. Sure, I lived in a home with lovely parents who bought me lovely things and loved me dearly. But something was missing inside me—that little part that keeps everyone else grounded and emotionally tied to this Earth. For me, that part was void. It never existed in the first place, so I hadn't been able to grow or nurture it like everyone else. In me, there were no feelings of hope or excitement. I did not envision children or a spouse or a kickass career.

All I could think about was what color the inside of my coffin would be. Would my parents splurge and get me a ridiculous silk–lined, wooden box that caused them to tap into their retirement? Or would they just use their credit card and buy the midgrade one—the one that has a thin padding and scratchy material but looks good enough on the outside?

I didn't plan on staying there anyway. They could have cremated me if that had been more in their budget. I'd have been happy with my remains sitting on the mantel next to Granny's and our dog, Buckie. It honestly wouldn't have mattered because I figured I would be running full force into the afterlife that awaited me. Something deep inside me knew I was better mentally equipped for that next phase. A part of me twitched and fidgeted at the idea of what was to come.

Was that what these other brainless drones called hope?

Dare I say I was hopeful?

Then it was all ruined.

One smile. One goddamned beautiful smile infected my heart and soul with such a force that I nearly exploded. All hopes of afterlife and the eagerness to leave this one vanished with that one handsome smile.

Thump.

My heart gave one painful thud and began beating for the first time in its life. I hated the feeling. Hated that the powers that be had realized I was onto their game. They made me their project. They showed me a smile. I was diseased by light from such a simple gesture.

Surely I could manage to look away and remember my goals. There had to be a way to avoid the magnetic glow that sucked me right in.

And then he spoke.

The beautiful smile had an even more beautiful voice. And with each word, each joke, and, eventually, each touch, I intertwined my soul so intricately with his that I never had a chance of letting go.

I fell in love.

And suddenly, life wasn't long enough.

Chapter One

Alpha

TODAY IS FA DAY—THE DAY WHEN ALL OF US Minders take on our final assignments before advancing to Seraph Guardians and getting our wings. I've wanted to be an SG since the moment I was recruited to HEA Corp.

Six years ago, I woke up with no recollection of my past. I'd been killed or died in some traumatic way but had "heroic qualities" according to my recruiting officer, Pallas, which is why I was recruited by HEA. That day, I showed up alongside Omega. They partnered us up, and we've been inseparable ever since.

Minders like Omega and I don't need sleep. We

don't require any sustenance like food and water. Minders also don't care about love or hate, right or wrong. Those of us who find ourselves in this position care about one thing: protecting those fragile, earthly beings they call humans. Since we were also human at one time, being a Minder is the step before becoming the ultimate badass, an SG. All Minders strive to become SGs. Unfortunately, not all Minders become them. Sometimes, they can't cut it and are sent next door for work.

Most Minders take decades to complete their assignments because they either fail or get more assignments as more required training. Omega and I, like a well-oiled wheel, are like the Tango and Cash of the afterlife. Our assignments come easily to us, and we have a great time completing them. When on assignment, we work together like two halves of a whole, which is why we're kicking ass and taking names. The other Minders, especially Herra and Loper, are jealous bastards, but they can't do a damn thing about it. And if they get too mouthy, HEL Enterprises is always at our doorsteps looking for new hires.

Omega and I often converse to see if we were brothers or best friends in our prior human bodies, but neither of us can remember and Pallas refuses to tell us. It only makes sense that we knew each other. Two people can't be that close upon instant meeting. There was a bond and a deep trust neither of us could pinpoint the origin to. Regardless, we held on to that bond and strengthened it over the past six years. I'd die for Omega—*if* I could die, that is.

The biggest downfall of becoming a Minder is the memory loss. You wake up in a body that doesn't belong to you, talking in a voice that was never yours, with a blank memory. For most, it isn't a big deal. Omega gives me shit about caring who the old me was. Something in my brain, though, won't allow me to give up. It is against our laws to discover who we were, and we aren't supposed to try. But I'll always wonder. And when I become an SG, I'll have the resources to find out.

"Ready for this, Al?" Omega's voice thunders as we tromp down the marbled hallway sounding like a herd of elephants.

"Brother, I was born ready. Pallas can bring on his toughest shit and I'll handle it with finesse," I joke as I slide my fingers through my longish, inky-black hair.

Omega calls my hair The Chick Magnet. The female Minders in our sector go batshit crazy over my hair. Minders don't care about their own looks. We actually avoid mirrors at all costs. Vanity isn't something we're allowed to think about—seven deadly sins and all—but we do care about the looks of others. Apparently, I'm what the females call "a hottie." Omega tells me all the time that it isn't fair that I got The Chick Magnet hair and he got lame, chocolate curls. He reminds me of a male model I had to once protect on assignment. The females here call Omega dreamy.

Hottie and Dreamy.

We kick ass and we're good-looking motherfuckers too. This life is a pretty sweet one, I tell you.

"Good luck, boys," Lovenia purrs as she stands outside the door of Pallas's office.

Omega lets an animalistic growl loose and I chuckle. Those two have it so bad for each other, but neither is making any steps to move forward. There's so much sexual tension between them that, when they finally do climb into the sack together, both Heaven and Hell will weep with joy because, quite frankly, we're all just over it.

Lovenia is a Leviathan. Try saying that three times fast. She's a higher-up at HEL Enterprises but likes slumming it with us when she's not on assignment. Our buildings are side by side, and our companies are sister companies. Employees of HEA work their way up. Literally. The higher the floor in our building, the more powerful you are at this company. HEL works just the opposite. Their head honcho, Luc, offices in the basement. They tell me it's hot there.

"You don't need luck when you're the Alpha and Omega duo. Luck needs us, baby," I grin and then wink at her.

She blushes and bats those long, dark lashes at me. Lovenia is all curves and smart as a whip, and she will lance you to bits with her sharp Latina tongue. Big, tough Omega will be handcuffed to her bed soon—it's only a matter of time. I may be a huge flirt, but I don't mess around too much on their side. It isn't against the Minder rules, but it is against SG policy. I figure the less I commingle with them, the better. My goals are big, so I can't let anyone or anything stand in my way.

"Hey, Omega. Why don't you come by my place after you get your FA and I'll give you a special treat," she speaks seductively to my partner.

The low growl in his throat is one of pure

want. If he wants to fuck her before becoming an SG, that'll be his only chance. I know my boy. He already has her naked in his head.

"I have a treat of my own for you, sweet Love," he smirks back.

She beams beautifully at his nickname for her, and for a second, I wonder if he'll back out on FA day just to haul her back to his quarters. They hold each other's heated stares before she approaches him and pecks him on the cheek.

"I'll be waiting in nothing but a big, red bow tied around my hips. You better hurry back and unwrap your gift," she says in a manner that could bring any man to his knees. Good thing my brother isn't human.

"Move it along, princess. We have work to do," I grumble in faux annoyance.

She giggles all the way down the hallway as she leaves us to take our final assignment before becoming true guardian angels. My mother would be proud—if I actually had one.

Omega strides up to Pallas's door and knocks loudly. Pallas is a partially deaf SG officer. Word on the street is he lost his hearing on his FA before becoming an SG. They don't speak much of their assignments because they are intended to be classified. But, even though we're angels in training, we're not perfect. The gossip mill is a quiet yet powerful machine. It doesn't help that most Leviathans are behind every rumor, whether it be truth or myth.

"Come in," Pallas hollers through the thick, wooden door.

Omega turns the knob and pushes through the opening. Instantly, we're hit with the stench of cigars. Good ol' Pallas has one permanently affixed between his yellow teeth, it would seem. Not once have I ever seen him take it out in the six years I've known him.

"Sit, boys," the gravelly voiced officer instructs.

We sit side by side and eagerly await our assignment. My leg has begun to bounce with contained energy that's just waiting to explode. This time in our life is do or die. We either pass or fail this final assignment. Passing means promotion and wings. Failing means termination from HEA Corp. Failure is not an option because I'd die before ever working for the other side which is exactly what would happen.

"First of all, I want to tell you both how proud of you I am. When I stumbled upon you two, I knew you were special. The both of you are like sons of mine." He takes a minute to let that sink in. "That being said, your final assignment will be difficult. My commanding officers have studied both of your cases and found things to insert into your mission that could compromise your ability to perform. They have direct access to your prior life. Your weaknesses have been highlighted and will be turned against you."

Omega grunts, and I flit my eyes over to him. His dark-brown eyes are brooding. He senses something bad coming. And I'd be a fool if I didn't sense it too.

"We're Minders, not humans. I think we can manage. We've killed it on every other mission, boss. You know this," I tell Pallas. Something in my voice indicates my uncertainty, and I instantly hate that feeling.

Pallas groans as he spouts off his next piece. "Yes, you kept your subjects alive for the allotted time periods before the Reapers took them. That's to be commended. Neither of you has ever failed. But to be SG worthy, you have to be strong in any capacity."

So far, our jobs have been easy. They put us on a

subject that can't see or hear us. We watch their every move. When they walk into traffic, we surge our power to make cars brake. If they slip in the shower, we break their fall. A subject of mine once choked on a meatball while at home alone and I just blasted him on the back, hurtling the meat across the room. We protect them—mostly from themselves—until D Day, also known as Death Day.

When Death Day arrives, the minions over at HEL, called Reapers, swoop in and take them to their final destination. Lovenia says that it's like a vacation at a warm beach minus the water and way hotter. Doesn't sound too bad . . .

"Did you hear me?" Pallas grumbles, yanking my attention back to him.

Not missing a beat, I say, "So, you're telling us something changes in the way we do our job?"

"Exactly. Same rules apply as far as mirrors—stay away so you don't become weak. And in the instance you do become weak, find a church or Bible—you'll heal quickly."

Omega and I nod in response. Nothing new so far.

"Here's the deal, boys," Pallas groans. "You'll be human for this job."

Omega bursts from his chair in a furious blast and leans across the desk with his finger in Pallas's face. "You can't do that! We're about to become fucking guardian angels! What about our powers?"

He's outraged, and I can't help but feel slightly betrayed. Why train us one way and then send us out with no tools?

"Don't curse in my office. I should write you up for that," Pallas snaps and swats Omega's hand away.

"Sit down, buddy. We'll figure it out," I tell him and yank down on the back of his suit jacket. Then I nervously wipe my palms on the thighs even though I don't sweat. Must be an old habit from my prior life.

Once Omega has relaxed a bit in his chair, Pallas continues his instructions.

"You won't have your powers. In fact, by becoming human for that short time, you'll be susceptible to real-life inflictions that will carry over to when you are an SG or . . ." he trails off.

We know he means we'll become fucking Reapers if we don't pass this mission.

"Anyway," he continues, "that's how I got this hearing problem. Bar fight. Some prick hit me in the head with a barstool while I was trying to protect a pool shark I was in charge of. You can get injured, but you won't die. You're still immortal. But don't go getting your legs blown off or some wicked stuff like that. You'll be a worthless SG. Believe me—I had to prove my tail off that I could still be an SG even with a handicap. That, boys, is why I sit behind a desk versus being out there with the likes of you."

My mind spins at what he's telling us. Omega is boiling over with rage.

"So, we'll be stripped of our powers, visible to our charges, and faced with obstacles we struggled with while in our former human lives? How long are our assignments?" I question.

Where Omega is pissed, I'm impatient to get this started. Something deep within me bounces back and forth on each foot like a boxer eager to fight. I love challenges, and thus far, we've handled everything with ease. Nobody has died on either of our watches. HEL got their people and we got closer to becoming an SG.

"In a nutshell. You'll encounter some other 'obstacles' along the way—and by 'obstacles,' I mean a Leviathan will be assigned to the both of you to complicate things. Why do you think Lovenia was here?" he grumbles as if her very existence makes him cringe.

To the both of us?

"Wait. You said, 'To the both of us.' We're always in close proximity for our missions, but you make it sound like we'll be on the same one," I say slowly.

"What happens if Lovenia fails in distracting us?" Omega spouts out, interrupting me.

His sudden interest in her well-being frays my nerves a bit, but I try to ignore it. Omega is the more passionate of the two of us. I'm the level head and the final say. In the end, Omega always listens to me.

"Yes. Your missions are neighbors in an apartment building. You'll be staying in the apartment across the hall from them. And, Omega, Lovenia's superiors will handle her failures—it isn't anything for you to think twice about. Here are your files," he says, handing us each a thick, brown folder.

I open mine and see a black and white photo of a dark-haired woman with hollow, drug-hazed eyes paper clipped to the front. She's beautiful but lost, hence her making it onto an FA list. Only the truly fucked up get on our list. As I skim through her file, I look at the assignment duration—three months.

All of our other assignments have been less than a month. The length of time unnerves me.

"Why so long?" Omega growls out his question, mimicking my internal one.

Pallas sighs, "Just part of the challenge. Look, boys, if it were easy, everyone would be a Seraph Guardian. The good people of this Earth deserve to be protected by angels who don't fall into temptation, are strong during moments of weakness, and don't become attached. This is your final test. You've passed with flying colors thus far. Granted, you will be pushed, but the two of you are strong. You'll succeed—I know it. I wouldn't have recruited you otherwise."

I flop my file closed and look over at my angry partner, who has his own file clutched so tight that his knuckles are turning white.

"Anything else, boss?" I ask Pallas while keeping my eyes trained on Omega.

"Report back here weekly. Look out for each other. And, boys," he says gruffly, "make me proud."

Why do I feel as if this will be more difficult than either of us could ever imagine?

Chapter Two

Lark

THE THUMP OF MY NEIGHBOR'S BASS INFURIATES me as I stalk toward my apartment door after a long-ass shift at the tattoo shop. All I want to do is crawl into my bed and pass out. I dealt with a whiny-ass biker earlier who was at least six foot three and nearly three hundred pounds for five hours straight as I inked his ribs with the words "Badass Motherfucker" encased in a bed of skulls. The pussy cried while his biker bitch stroked his hair. I wanted to fucking puke, but I was making five hundred bucks on the deal and needed it to support my habit.

My habit.

The only thing that makes me smile in this godforsaken life.

I pull the keys from my worn purse and prepare to push them into the lock when I hear the music getting louder as Pedro emerges from his apartment.

Fuck.

"*Estás muy buena!*" he hollers as he stumbles his way toward me.

"Not tonight, asshole. I'm tired as hell, and for the thousandth time, I'm not going to sleep with you," I snarl as I whirl around to face him.

He's totally fucked up tonight, which sends a shiver skittering down my spine. I can hardly thwart his advances on a normal night, but when he's high on meth, it's nearly impossible because he is so damn persistent.

I attempt to turn the key in the lock with my eyes watching his every move. I'm not letting him out of my sight until the door slams in his face and I'm safely behind my locked front door.

"*Chupame la polla,*" he laughs like a fucking hyena as he thrusts his dick at me, using his hand to pretend he's holding the head of someone bobbing on his cock.

Sick.

"Buzz off, Pedro. I'm not fucking joking. Carlos already said if you caused any more trouble, he was going to evict your ass. Don't make me turn you in," I threaten.

Compared to Pedro, I'm a shrimp. I'm only five foot six and a hundred and ten pounds if I'm soaking wet. Pedro, who's fresh out of prison, has tattoos on his face for fucking crying out loud and wears wifebeaters five sizes too small. I'm no match for him in any way, shape, or form. The little knife on my key chain can barely open my mail, much less fillet the heart of a registered-sex-offender parolee.

I wrote a poem about his ass once and taped it to his door.

Pedro is built like a wall.
An ugly, graffiti, big
fucking wall.
So tall.
And solid.
But still, a big-ass wall.
If he thinks I'd ever
willingly crawl into bed
with his stinky ass,
He's got some balls.

Lark

I think he took it as some sort of advance on my part. I was just angry one night and felt like taking it out on my annoying-ass neighbor. The next morning, I blamed my moment of insanity on the vodka.

Oh, the vodka.

I only pull it out once a month on the eighteenth. The eighteenth has been the title of many poems. All of them were shredded and burned in a trash can after I cried big, ugly tears.

He holds up two fingers in a peace sign and sticks his tongue between it, licking provocatively at me. "*Te voy a hacer la sopa.*"

Enough already. "Goodbye, Pedro. Talk to me tomorrow when you're sober. And in English. Night," I groan. Then I mistakenly turn my back to him to twist the key and open my door.

The brief drop of my guard is just enough for the hardened criminal to pounce. His thick, strong arms encase me in a bear hug from behind. I can feel his erection stabbing me in the back.

"Let go!" I screech and squirm from his grasp.

He inhales my hair like a fucking lunatic. On the first, I am out of here. I don't know where I'll go, but I'm out of this hellhole. I'd rather live in box down by the river than next door to this freak any longer.

When he leans into me, my hand turns the knob on my door and we stumble inside. Shit! The last thing I need is for him to be in my place with me.

"*Te la voy a meter de mira quien viene,*" he hisses into my ear as he thrusts into my back a few times.

I'm attempting to wriggle from his grasp so I

can claw his fucking eyes out when he's suddenly ripped from me.

My eyes skim right past him to the man who makes Pedro look like a twelve-year-old boy. This man is beautiful in his thunderous glory. Black hair a little on the overgrown and wild side sticks out every which direction on the top of his head, giving him a mischievous look. His eyes nearly match that of his hair, and his angry brows are furrowed as his hand closes around the throat of my punk-ass neighbor.

"Just take him next door. When he isn't high as a kite, he's not too bad. No need to kill him," I grumble.

My words seem to alert him to me, and his head snaps to look my way. Something flashes behind his eyes, and I'm incredibly curious of the man before me.

"Are you hurt?" he asks in a voice so low that I swear it rumbles right through the walls of my own chest.

Instead of answering him, I drink up his features. Strong nose. Perfect, rosy lips. Scruffy jaw.

"Let him go, Al," a growl orders from behind him.

I burst into hysterical laughter as another gorgeous man steps into my apartment beside the god of a man before me.

"What's so funny?" Al demands angrily.

Tears stream down my cheeks. Damn, I haven't laughed this hard since . . .

"Al? Really? Big, badass demigod and your name is Al?" I finally choke out past my tears.

"I'm not a *demigod*," Al snarls as if the word is venom on his lips.

The man beside him chuckles and winks. "I'm *Omar*, and I'll take care of this guy for you."

Al's eyes remain furiously locked on mine as Omar grabs Pedro by the shirt and hauls him out of my apartment. Without my greasy neighbor between us, I fully take in the sight of him.

His olive-colored skin is flawless, and the artist within me twitches to paint that canvas. Rigid, defined muscles are encased in a tight, black T-shirt, and his jeans are dark and fitted. My eyes peruse his body without shame. When a body like this fills the entryway of your apartment, you take a moment to enjoy the beauty of it. Finally, I flit my eyes back to his, which remain fixed on my face.

"Like what you see?" he asks with a dark brow

raised. One corner of his mouth twitches, and I immediately look down at the floor.

Smiles get people in trouble. Smiles cause pain.

"Something like that. Thanks for showing up on your horse, Romeo, but I'm tired as hell. Catch you later?" I steal a glance at him, and the humor is gone as he watches me.

"My brother and I are moving into the apartment across the hall from that motherfucker. We'll keep you safe," he promises.

The way his words thunder on his last line—I feel it deep down in my soul. This man is completely serious. It will be kind of nice having someone like him around to help me contend with Pedro.

"Uh, thanks, Al," I giggle.

He looks like a Dominic or a Maximus. Maybe even a Sebastian. Something powerful and sexy. Not Al. Thoughts of Al Bundy with his hand in his pants on the show Married with Children infect my brain, and I give way to more hysterical laughter.

"Woman, are you crazy?" he asks, seeming to genuinely want to know the answer.

Yes. Certifiably so.

"Al, I'm the kind of crazy that makes insane look fun and inviting. My kind of crazy is on a whole new level."

Without warning, he stalks over to me and slides his hands into my long, thick, mahogany-colored hair. Then he tilts my head to look at him. Now that he's close, I can't help but inhale his utter masculinity. It's a scent that makes my tongue water with the desire to taste him.

"Do you ever eat?" he questions gruffly.

Hardly. When you live in a state of despair and depression, food is the last thing on your mind.

"Time to leave, Al."

His proximity is causing my heart to tense up, and I don't like the feeling. My breathing becomes shallow as I attempt to keep his smell out of my body, from infecting my very being.

When I feel his thumb stroke my jaw, my eyes flutter closed. I want to freeze this moment and live in it forever. Moments like this are rare for me. Moments where I feel free from it all.

"Promise me you'll eat more, woman."

My eyes reopen, and I smile. "Call me Lark. If you cook for me, maybe I'll eat more often."

His eyes leave mine to watch my mouth as I say my name. He seems lost in my lips. For the briefest of moments, I'd like his lips to get lost there too.

"I haven't cooked in years," he says thoughtfully. Dark eyes unwillingly leave my lips to stare deep into my green eyes.

My mouth quirks up in a half smile. "I haven't eaten in years."

His face darkens with anger—as if he knows and is pissed that I only eat ramen noodles and cereal. I can't help it though. When the mood strikes for me to eat, those are handy and easy. Although . . . my milk is usually expired and I end up whipping up ramen noodles, even for breakfast. My only vice—and truly what keeps me alive—are my Oreos. Double Stuf Oreos. Just one of my many habits . . .

"You're going to eat, baby, even if I have to spoon-feed that pretty little mouth," he flirts.

All seriousness is gone as we both break into simultaneous smiles at the idea of him feeding me.

Smiles.

Fuck.

Thump.

Made in USA - North Chelmsford, MA
1105141_9781534941229
05.12.2020 1647